I0580969

Other books by Deirdre Hutchins

The Paranormal Investigators League series

PIL #1 Voodoo in Savannah

PIL #2 A Hanging in Tucson

PIL #3 Suicide on Sunset

PIL #4 The Legend of Providence

PIL #5 Darkness in Denver

PIL Prequel: The Origin Story

The Dark Prophecy trilogy

1: Resurrection of the Vampire

2: Vengeance of the Damned

These are all available from the San Joaquin Valley Press.

Visit us at www.sanjoaquinvalleypress.com

The Dark Prophecy

Book 2: Vengeance of the Damned

A Novel about Vampires and Witches

By Deirdre Hutchins

San Joaquin Valley Press
Fresno, California

ISBN 978-1-7378061-3-4

1

It was a beautiful, clear Southern California night. Luke and Shane stood side by side staring at the dirt. It had been two nights since they had buried Kara, the stepdaughter of their sworn enemy, here in this very place.

Shane was nervous and excited, like a farmer waiting for eggs to hatch in the spring. Only Shane wasn't sure what he was going to do with her once he had her. Would she be a loyal vampire? Or would her relation to the witches pull her back to them?

"Are you two proud papas going to be out here all night?" Isabelle came out to the patio to watch them. Isabelle was a proud vampire warrior, one of the fiercest Shane had ever seen. He was proud that she was on his side. That—and he definitely wouldn't want to be her enemy. If it weren't for his ability to control certain elements, she would beat him in hand-to-fang combat every time.

"This could be the night," Shane explained without turning around. He tried to sound calm and collected, but there was a waiver of nervousness to his voice.

"Yeah. Or it could be tomorrow or the next day. Or the next day. You can't not hunt for a week waiting for her. Go feed and I'll keep watch," Isabelle instructed in her bossy way. Her long, dark hair was up in a ponytail and she was wearing her black boots she loved to use when she rode her Ducati. She presented herself as someone not to be messed with.

Shane shook his head. "I'm not leaving."

Luke turned back to Isabelle and flashed his Hollywood perfect smile. "And I'm her sire, so I need to be here when she resurrects."

Isabelle folded her arms across her chest. "And I like to watch dumbasses do dumbass shit, so I guess we're all here all night."

With his eyes still locked on the loosely turned dirt at his feet, Shane gestured at the patio table behind him. "Pull up a seat."

Isabelle hated being told what to do, so she remained standing just to be defiant. "As long as we're all going to be out here staring at a pile of dirt, can I talk to you about some business, Shane?"

"As if I could stop you, Isabelle," Shane smirked.

Isabelle couldn't suppress the grin that danced across her face. She loved the way he respected her toughness. "Okay. First, regarding your witch—"

This got Shane's attention. Swinging his eyes from the dirt and straight to Isabelle he asked, "Camilla? Is she all right?"

"Relax, lover boy. I haven't killed her. Yet." Isabelle half-smiled. She was only half-kidding.

"Ha, ha," Shane responded sardonically and turned back to the unmoving dirt.

"She's a pain in the ass," Isabelle explained.

"So are you, but we still love you." Luke winked at Isabelle and she fought the urge to punch him. A hard right straight to the gut would double him over and wipe that pretty-boy smile right off those handsome lips.

She made a face at Luke but moved on. "She doesn't belong in a vampire compound. Besides the fact that someone's probably going to get hungry and feed on her, she could be spying for Theresa this whole time."

Shane sighed. He'd heard it all before. Even though his sixth sense gave him the intuition to know that Camilla was telling the truth about choosing them over the Harbor Coven, no one else knew that. "It isn't like you to be coy. Get to the point, Isabelle."

Isabelle took a step closer. "You need to turn her."

Shane snapped his neck he responded so quickly to Isabelle. Her words had caught him by surprise, which wasn't easy to do. He closed the gap between them and Isabelle stood her ground. Their mutual respect for one another made them each confident that the other wouldn't hurt them. Even though both could hurt the other easily. Isabelle could rip his throat out with one swift swipe, but Shane could burn her to a crisp with a snap of his fingers.

He didn't lay a finger on her, but she could tell he was upset. "I'm not turning her against her will."

"It's honestly the right thing to do, Shane. Think about it. If she's truly loyal to us, she shouldn't mind being turned." Isabelle was passionate about this. But so was Shane.

"Isabelle," Luke interjected. "You do know there are other emotions besides wanting to kill someone all the time? You can see he cares about the girl."

Isabelle's face softened. Her eyes glanced from Luke to Shane. "Yes. I can see that. Believe it or not, that's why I am saying it."

"And believe me or not, I know Camilla is no threat despite where she came from. She stays. Untouched," Shane fumed. "Anyone who dares to harm her will answer to me."

"Then I'll be her protector. Her bodyguard," Isabelle said, swallowing. She would have to fight the instinct to murder Camilla at every turn, but she would do it out of her loyalty for Shane.

"I'll do it," a sweet voice shouted from the sliding glass door that led to the patio. The three vampires turned to see the angelic face of Camilla, her brown hair twisted and draped along her left shoulder. She stepped out onto the patio to join them. "I'll become a vampire. If that's what you all need to believe me."

"We believe you," Shane said with lowered eyes and a voice two octaves lower than normal.

Camilla smiled as she walked toward the vampires huddled near the patch of overturned dirt. Her smile was like the sun's rays, warming Shane's heart and causing him to want to put her in some kind of bubble where no one could ever harm her.

It had the opposite effect on Isabelle. Camilla's smile made Isabelle think of a predator lying in wait. Luke just watched the scene unfold. He was skeptical of witches in general, but he trusted Shane's judgment.

"*You* believe me, but no one else does." Camilla glanced over at Isabelle. "And I don't blame them. I wouldn't believe me either if the roles were reversed."

Shane reached a hand to Camilla and she clasped his willingly, but before Shane could say any soothing words, Isabelle blurted out, "Why? Why are you here?"

"Isabelle," Shane growled, but Camilla laid a warm hand on his chest.

"It's okay." Camilla smiled but it was a weak smile. It looked like someone sad and lost who just needed a kindness. "I'm sure it sounds strange to all of you, but I've never had a choice before. It actually feels good to choose this."

Isabelle crossed her arms across her chest, lips tight. "You honestly expect us to believe you joined a witch's coven against your will?"

"I don't know how to make anyone believe anything. I'm not Theresa." Camilla let out a nervous laugh. "But it's the truth." She looked straight into Shane's eyes. "I was a normal sixteen-year-old girl when Theresa found me. I had a family that loved me and friends who supported me."

Camilla's eyes turned to Luke's. "Theresa lures

you in with promises of eternity and riches. And I suppose all that's true. I snuck around willingly at first, joining weekly gatherings. Drinking potions, bathing in blood. I was a teenager and it felt good to do something so bad. Rebellious."

Camilla then turned to Isabelle, pleading in her eyes. "But eventually the newness wore off and I was tired of sneaking around all the time. I tried to stop coming to the coven gatherings and Theresa dragged me there by my hair. Not long after that she moved to Ventura and I was forced to come along. I never saw my family again."

She turned back to Shane, reaching for him. He held her hands tight. "She told me my family would never accept me back now that I was a pawn of the devil. And I knew that was true. I'm from a conservative Christian family in a small town in North Carolina. I couldn't ever go back and tell them what I had done. So I was stuck."

"Living on the streets?" Luke asked, questioning in his eyes, but not accusatory.

"No. Theresa calls us 'family,' although it's a twisted one at best," Camilla explained. "She found me a foster home until I turned eighteen. Then she got me an apartment and gave me a job at her salon. As long as I worked there and came to the coven gatherings, I was in her good graces."

"And now?" Isabelle asked.

Camilla looked at her hands entwined with Shane's. She took a deep breath before answering. "Well, now I can't go back. I'm as good as dead if I do." She looked up at Isabelle. "I'm as good as dead even here. So you might as well make me a vampire like you did Kara. Then both her little pets can be her sworn enemy."

"You don't have to do anything out of fear of Theresa." Shane tucked Camilla in under his arm and pulled her close, kissing her forehead. "She'll never lay a finger on you again."

"What if you help us with intel?" Luke stepped forward. "Maybe we don't have to go to extremes here. If you help us—give us information to bring down

Theresa—people will believe your loyalty without you having to die and be reborn as a vampire."

Camilla nodded vigorously and then looked from Luke up toward Shane. "I can do that easily. I know everything about her."

"I still find it hard to believe you were a witch against your will," Isabelle said rolling her eyes, "but I'm willing to give you a chance to redeem yourself." Isabelle stepped forward, strong and tough in her black leather boots. She looked murderous. "But if you break Shane's heart, I will kill you."

"Isabelle!" Shane shouted.

"I promise you I will." Isabelle stood there fuming.

Camilla nodded and swallowed hard. "I believe you."

"Okay, Isabelle, we get it." Luke grabbed her arms and pulled her back away from the pretty little witch. "Your scare tactics are always effective. But let's just enjoy the peaceful evening now, shall we?"

Luke emulated Shane and tucked Isabelle under

his arm. To his surprise, she didn't pull away or punch him. She just stood there and let him hold her, listening to the crickets in the distance. The night was calm, peaceful. He had braced himself for an attack that never came.

Instead, he heard the silence of the evening broken by a scratching at his feet.

Luke looked straight at Shane and both their eyes widened.

The dirt at their feet was moving.

Luke sprang into action first, digging the dirt away. Shane had never been on this side of the event in his reborn life, so he copied Luke and began moving dirt by the handful.

Camilla and Isabelle watched silently, a kind of nervous excitement again filling the air.

From elbows deep in fresh dirt, Luke turned to Shane. "Isn't there a faster way to do this, oh mighty Chosen One?"

Shane looked down at his soiled hands. He hadn't tried to move dirt yet, but if he could control fire, water and wind, it seemed likely that the power was within him. He closed his eyes and used the same part of his mind he used to control other elements. He called to the dirt and pulled it off the newborn vampire buried beneath him.

Luke, Camilla and Isabelle watched mountains of dirt fly away seemingly on their own and land on the grass a few feet away.

"Thanks." Luke slapped a hand on Shane's back, and Shane opened his eyes to see a small hand reaching up to the sky.

Shane and Luke both reached down and helped Kara out of the dirt. Suddenly, Shane had a flash to his rebirth and the first face he had seen. It had been that of the sister he had long thought was dead. His heart squeezed at the memory of Julianna's beautiful face. He remembered confusion, and running, and frustration. He wanted Kara's first day to be much smoother and easier.

"Don't be afraid," Shane said calmly.

Kara, covered in dirt and, staring darkly through

angry eyes, extended her fangs. She looked vicious and nothing like Shane had expected. "I'm hungry," she growled.

2

"I just don't believe it." Richard stared blankly at the ocean in front of him. He was holding his coffee in his hand but hadn't touched a drop. He hadn't eaten much in a few days. "I can't believe Kara would just run away like that."

Theresa stepped through the large sliding glass window that connected their dining room to the oceanfront patio, joining her husband at the railing. She put her arms around his waist in an effort to comfort him or distract him. A week ago, he would have lovingly held her in his arms. Now he barely registered her presence and continued staring at the ocean. Even Theresa's love potions were barely working.

"You know how teenagers are," Theresa said with a smile, trying to sound as casual as possible. "I'm sure she'll be back when she realizes how good she had it here." Even though she knew good and well that if Kara ever came back, she'd probably murder her own father and lick his blood off her lips.

"I should be out looking for her, but I don't know where she would have gone." Richard spoke the words mechanically, like a robot, his eyes still glued to the sea. "I was supposed to take care of her. Keep her happy and safe. And I failed."

He didn't say it so much as someone who was preoccupied with safety as much as someone who wasn't used to failing at something he set out to do.

"First Margaret, now Kara." He shook his head at the memory of his wife's death. How had it taken Kara's disappearance to make him feel guilty for Margaret's death? He had failed them both. Of course, he had no way of knowing that the woman next to him had really been the cause of the demise of both women. If Theresa had never seen him that day, they'd both be here alive and well. But he had no idea who Theresa really was, so he continued blaming himself.

Theresa rubbed his back in small circles. Maybe she should've just wiped his memory of Kara. She could wipe his memory of Margaret too. But she had decided against it, partially because she knew she and Emily might slip up and mention them one day, causing real confusion. And also, she thought it was cruel. He had lost a wife and a daughter and he deserved to mourn them. Theresa had never had any animosity toward Margaret—she'd just been in her way. And Kara she'd actually cared for. She even had a soft spot for Richard. "There, there. She *is* happy. She chose to run off with... *that boy.*"

"I should call his parents." Richard turned to Theresa, for the first time even really acknowledging her presence. He grabbed her shoulders, none too gently she noticed. "Do you still have the note?"

Theresa was quickly fleshing out the lie when Emily walked out onto the patio with her father and stepmother.

"Theresa's right," Emily stated, her chin held high. She was well-dressed and had make-up on, which was not unusual for Emily. But, Theresa noticed, there was an air of sophistication that hadn't been there before Kara's death. She suddenly looked older, more mature. "Kara told me the day before she left that she was moving to downtown Los Angeles with Braden."

Emily looked right at Theresa, and they exchanged the look of two women in cahoots. Theresa nodded in return, appreciating Emily's support.

Richard's jaw dropped and then his face turned red. He stormed inside and plopped his still-full coffee cup on the counter. "And you didn't tell me this until now? Grab your stuff! We're going after her."

In his disheveled robe, and his hair tousled from the windy patio, he slipped on his tennis shoes with no socks and grabbed his car keys from the counter where they lay inches from his sloshing coffee cup.

Theresa reached for him lovingly. She had always handled him this way, like a pet or a toy she enjoyed playing with. Emily, truly unlike herself, stepped in front of him with her arms folded. She had never talked back to anyone in her life. She'd always been the dismissive one. Now she looked like an army general.

"No, dad." She stared him down and he stood there, probably stunned by her behavior. "You can't go after her. She'll only run further. You have to let her have this and she'll come home when she's ready, just like Theresa said."

Richard's shoulders slumped. He didn't look entirely convinced that he shouldn't go after Kara, but he didn't argue with Emily either.

"Drink your orange juice, honey." Theresa handed him the orange juice she gave him every morning, spiked with the love potion that kept him devoted to her. She smiled as warmly as she ever had, still trying to play wife despite the situation.

Without making eye contact or saying a single word, Richard grabbed the glass of orange juice from Theresa and walked over to the sink and poured it down the drain.

Theresa and Emily watched him as he then made his way in a zombie-like fashion down the hallway, presumably back to bed. He hadn't gone to work—hell, he hadn't even gotten dressed—in days.

Emily spoke in a harsh whisper to her stepmother. "You've got to fix him. This is ridiculous. Now he's going to wander the streets of Los Angeles looking for Kara."

"All I can do is wipe his memory and make him forget, and that doesn't seem fair to Kara's memory," Theresa whisper-yelled back.

"You need to fix this." Emily stood inches from Theresa's face with a confidence Theresa had never seen before. Standing up to the leader of the Harbor Coven? Perhaps there was hope for Emily, after all.

Theresa softened. She had lost Kara, but she could now see that maybe there was a way she could get a witch out of this family despite the recent turn of events. "Forget your dad. He's the least of our worries. If you really want to honor your sister's memory, meet me at the warehouse in half an hour."

Theresa left to get dressed, humming as she went. She'd never believed in getting mad if you could get even. And she intended to get even with those bastard vampires if it was the last thing she did on this earth.

Emily watched Theresa exit the kitchen and knew with every fiber of her being that she'd be joining her stepmother at the witch's lair. A week ago, the most important thing in her life had been making the varsity cheer squad. Suddenly, she saw the world for what it was. Darkness and light. Spotlight and shadows. Good and evil. Her stepmother was evil, she was certain of that. Had Emily been good? Maybe. But now she had made the decision to become a witch and dedicate her life to the family business: murdering vampires.

If she had to, she might even kill Kara. If she was going to choose evil, she might as well choose it.

The thought of her sister as one of those hideous monsters made her stomach turn. She remembered how the vampires had kidnapped Kara and Emily that night, controlling them and overpowering them, all just to use the sisters to make Theresa surrender. They would pay for that. With an even greater resolve, Emily hopped in her car and drove to Theresa's salon. She would wait in the warehouse patiently. She would wait for her chance to sell her soul and get revenge.

Other Harbor Coven witches started filing in shortly after Emily. They greeted Emily with a smile, truly grateful that she was with them. More witches meant a stronger coven, and young fresh blood was always invigorating.

In the middle of the warehouse, a table had been set up with a body lying underneath a white sheet. Emily wasn't one-hundred percent certain who was under there, but she thought she had a good idea and the thought warmed her heart. And then the joy of causing someone else the pain that she had felt made her feel guilty. But she swallowed it down. She had decided to become a witch. And while she knew very little about what that actually meant, she was positive that witches didn't feel guilt over causing their enemies pain.

Some witches began stripping down, removing every article of clothing and then chanting weird incantations that sounded foreign to Emily's ears. She watched in awe, not sure if she was supposed to join them or not. Other witches hung around, seemingly waiting for Theresa's instructions.

And when she arrived, her entrance could not remain unnoticed. Theresa swept in through the red door that connected the warehouse to the salon and every voice became silent. Every movement stopped, save for the turning of heads in her direction. She was an irresistible force, pulling the witches' attention straight to her. Even Emily found herself holding her breath, and she lived with the woman.

Theresa sauntered across the floor, her hair pulled back in a tight bun, her pencil skirt moving tight across her legs, her high heels clickety-clacking on the industrial floor. As if no one else were in the room, Theresa stormed straight to Emily, a smile creeping across her lips.

"You've chosen well." Theresa couldn't hide her delight. "But you cannot unsee what you are about to see. Are you prepared for this?"

"Theresa,"—Emily tried to make her voice sound as full of conviction as she felt—"I don't just want to watch. I want to participate."

A murmur broke out amongst the other coven members. Theresa glanced at them briefly and then smiled more widely at her stepdaughter. "Only witches can do the ceremony. What exactly are you saying?"

Emily swallowed and then locked eyes purposefully with Theresa. There was no going back once she said the words. But, really, she felt there was no going back after the fateful night in the mountains. She couldn't restore her innocence. "I want to join your coven."

Elyse was the first to run to Emily's side and congratulate her with a hug. Other witches began to come to her, laughter and joy bubbling throughout.

Theresa stopped them with the raising of one hand. "You realize that this means you have to make a covenant with the devil himself? You have to pledge yourself to the dark magic and bathe yourself in blood."

Emily heard her words and thought about them.

Would she ever be able to go back to a "normal" life? No. Did she want to see herself bitten and sucked dry by a vampire? No. Did she feel a seed of power taking hold at the thought of using "dark magic," as Theresa had called it, to destroy her enemies? Yes.

Emily nodded. "I'll do it."

As the witches of Harbor Coven cackled with glee, Theresa stared skeptically at her stepdaughter. Emily? A witch? The girl who never once cheated on a math test? Emily, who had never once kissed a boy? A kernel of darkness must have always been deep in her soul in order to sprout now. And Theresa knew better than anyone how traumatic events can trigger that. Hadn't she become a witch in the first place to save her own mother's life?

"Very well," Theresa responded, walking over to the shelves behind Emily and Elyse. She pulled out two black robes. "Before we resurrect the asshole's sister," (that's how Theresa had begun referring to Shane now—the asshole) "we'll watch Emily take the pledge."

Emily felt her pulse quicken. She was part

excited, part nervous, but determined all the way. Theresa handed her a black robe and Emily emulated her stepmother's actions as they both donned the robes and pulled the hoods up over their heads.

Theresa gestured toward the middle of the warehouse. "Center of the circle, please." Emily turned to see the witches of Harbor Coven already gathered in a circle next to, but not encompassing, 'the asshole's' sister. Emily went to the middle, unsure of what to expect.

Theresa quickly combined bay leaves with taro root in the witch's potion, splashing it with a final dash of rat tail and giving it a stir. It smoked and fizzled as it was supposed to. Theresa grabbed the grimoire and walked over to Emily with a sense of pride. She'd always wanted to have a witch in the family. Losing Kara had been a blow to her plans, something she didn't take lightly. But perhaps it could still be salvaged.

"Read these words aloud and then drink this potion. All of it," Theresa instructed. "My youngest witch, Camilla, will take you under her wing and train you on the basics. Camilla!"

Theresa scanned the faces of the circle and the other witches looked around nervously. Theresa locked eyes with Elyse when they realized Camilla was not among them

"Where the hell is Camilla?!" Theresa shrieked.

3

"When I was a newborn vampire, I was trained by my sire to find victims at a bar. It's the best place," Shane instructed Kara, his eyes on the front door of the bar. Luke stood on Kara's other side, both men mentoring her in the ways of being a vampire. They were in the shadows of the evening, but not completely out of sight. "Above all, you must control yourself and be discreet."

"Discreet my ass," Kara grumbled and stepped into the street, crossing toward the bar, traffic be damned.

Luke looked at Shane with an eyebrow raised. "This girl's going to give Isabelle a run for her money."

Kara stopped under the glow of a streetlamp.

She didn't exactly look seductive or enthralling. She looked like a homeless teenager, still dirty from her resurrection, her blonde hair wild and unbrushed. But she knew what she wanted and didn't seem at all fazed by what she was about to do.

She was a far cry from Shane at this point in his second life.

Two drunk men stumbled toward her, laughing and pointing in her direction. Shane and Luke watched from across the street, curious what Kara would do but ready to jump in at a moment's notice if needed. Luke didn't think she'd need them in the slightest.

Kara smiled coyly, lifting a shoulder as if she were flirting. This made the drunk men laugh even more. She stepped forward slowly and one of the men rubbed her arm as if he were making an advance. She reached up slowly, cupping his face. He smiled, leaning in for a kiss. She closed the distance between them, standing on her tiptoes and moving her lips to within a hair's breadth of his. At the last moment she turned his head with a sudden jolt and sank her fangs deep into his neck, piercing the carotid with pinpoint accuracy.

Realizing that something wasn't right, the other drunk man began to run. Shane started toward him, but Kara was faster. She dropped the first guy in an unconscious heap and grabbed the second guy, throwing him up against the wall. He screamed, but it was short-lived as she ripped his neck open, drinking him until he collapsed.

She went back to the first guy and finished him off, leaving him a shriveled-up corpse with no fluid inside.

Shane stood in the gutter and flicked his wrist, burning both bodies to ash and eliminating the evidence. Kara watched and wiped her mouth with the back of her hand.

"Will you teach me to do that?" Kara asked.

"I don't know if I can," Shane answered honestly.

From across the street, Luke came toward them, clapping loudly. "Nicely done, Kara."

She smiled and took a bow dramatically. Shane just shook his head.

"You are a born predator," Luke smiled and shook his head. "Two guys your first night out? With no help? And no hesitation? I am impressed."

"You guys do this every night?" Kara asked with a wicked gleam in her eye.

"Well, not necessarily every night. But we have to feed," Luke explained.

"I usually try to choose bad people, so I don't have a guilty conscience," Shane explained, trying again to mold his young protégé.

"Why?" Kara asked with honest surprise. "Does the lion feel guilty when he eats a gazelle?"

Luke laughed. "I like her."

"Well," Shane said with a sigh, "we may not have a choice in being vampires, but we can choose not to be monsters."

Kara shrugged. "So next time I'll eat without killing anyone. I don't think we're monsters if we eat what we were made to eat." Her tone was casual, as if they were discussing the pros and cons of eating ice cream rather than human blood. She turned to Luke, a huge smile on her face. "What now, Lukey?"

"Now, we go home," Shane announced with a frown. He wasn't sure what a night on the town with Kara would be, and he wasn't sure he was ready to find out. *And did she just call their companion Lukey?*

"We can't take her home yet. She's a young sparrow who's just learned to fly," Luke pleaded with Shane. Shane had known nothing but backstabbing and intrigue since he'd been born, but Luke had known a lifetime of freedom and immortality. "You could use a night out, too, my young, powerful friend. The sun won't come up for hours and, for once, no one is trying to kill you."

Shane fought the early signs of a smile as he thought about a night of fun. When had he gotten so old and boring? He'd only been on this earth twenty years. A flash of a memory of himself on a surfboard, wind tousling his hair, entered his mind and reminded him of carefree human days. He hadn't always been a fuddy duddy. Why was he fighting with someone three hundred years his senior?

"Please, Shaney," Kara pouted dramatically, her fangs still extended. "It's my first night as a vampire. Let's celebrate!"

Luke tugged the sleeve of Shane's black trench coat. "Come on. I have an idea."

With an undercurrent of foreboding, Shane answered sarcastically, "This should be interesting."

Kara slipped her arm in Shane's and they followed Luke back into the shadows. With their vampire speed, they were in the mountains within five minutes. These mountains, Shane realized, were the ones he had come through with Julianna on his first night as a vampire. She'd been so sure he was the one from the Dark Prophecy—a prophecy that hadn't even been real. Shane had never been that sure of anything in his whole life.

The memory of his sister's death flashed in his head yet again, and he shook it from his mind.

"Are we here to kill wildlife?" Kara asked optimistically.

Luke laughed. "I can't decide if I should pair you

up with Isabelle right away or keep you two far apart."

"And what were you thinking by bringing us up here, Luke?" Shane asked.

"I thought we could teach Kara to fight. The basics anyway." Luke turned back toward Kara and Shane, facing them now from a few feet up the mountain. "And more importantly, I think you should cut loose with your powers without having to prove anything to anyone."

"I cut loose sometimes," Shane argued, but he didn't sound convincing even to his own ears. Luke said nothing but raised an eyebrow in return.

"Since you love the hunt, Kara," Luke began, "you two can hunt me." Without waiting for a response, he sped off into the night. Shane looked at Kara and decided to roll with it. He gestured for Kara to go ahead of him and, with a gleam in her eye, she took off at top speed in the same direction Luke had just gone. Shane shook his head, but then decided to play along. He figured he might as well try to 'cut loose.' He took off, following the path Kara had blazed at top speed.

The tall grass and occasional tree branch whizzed by in a blur as he sped up the mountain in the direction Kara had gone. When he reached the top, he paused, scanning the mountain top. Before him lay a large valley. Behind him, he could see the Pacific Ocean. Nowhere did he see Luke or Kara. He closed his eyes and used his heightened hearing. A slight rustle of leaves off to his left was the only sound he heard. It could have been an animal, but he heard nothing else and his gut told him he was right.

As he bolted off to the left, he took in a deep breath of air through his nose, alert to all the scents coming from that direction. Fresh grass, wildflowers, and dirt mixed with blood.

Kara.

He knew he was getting closer as the scent got stronger. He ran faster and faster, the ground barely touching his feet. He wondered what she was doing to Luke if she'd caught up with him.

The sound of rustling had stopped, replaced by the sound of something flying quickly through the air.

He slowed in time to see a spear flying at him at top speed. With hardly time to react before the spear pierced him in the chest, Shane called on his fire power and burnt the spear to a crisp.

A sound of complete elation was followed by a celebratory shout from Luke. The two of them were standing a football field's length away, jumping up and down and squealing with joy at Shane's small show of power.

"Is that all you've got?" Shane shouted.

"You wish!" And Luke took off running toward Shane at full speed. He was hunched low as he ran, as if he planned to tackle him when he got there. Extending his claws and fangs as he ran, Luke prepared for the attack.

Shane rolled his eyes and flicked his wrist at Luke and Luke flew backward as if he'd hit a brick wall. Kara laughed again, jumping up and down some more and looking very much like the fourteen-year-old-girl she was. When he stopped rolling, Luke shouted to Kara. "Plan B!"

Instantly, her eyes turned murderous and she crouched as if preparing to launch herself at someone.

"Oh really, Luke? Now you're going to send the little girl?" Shane shouted.

Kara and Luke exchanged a look, and then they both took off toward Shane at top speed. Kara was flanking his left, Luke on his right. Part of Shane wanted to engage, to fight just as Isabelle had taught him. He knew Luke wasn't a supreme fighter and Kara was hours old. He thought for once he might have a chance at victory.

But he knew they were only toying with him. They just wanted to see his display of power. He was supposed to be "cutting loose," after all.

So he folded his arms and closed his eyes. He concentrated on the dirt beneath their feet and the hillside began to roll, coming at Luke and Kara like a tidal wave made of earth. Kara watched it closely and as the rolling earth came toward her, she tried to jump out of its way, but there was nowhere to go. The ground in every direction was rolling in waves, as if it were the ocean. The earth picked her up and carried her away from Shane. She was powerless to overcome it.

Luke, on the other hand, was diving over the waves of earth, laughing as he did. He wasn't getting far fast, but he wasn't being carried away from Shane either. Shane laughed at Luke as they locked eyes. He had an idea—and Luke could see it on his face.

Shane concentrated again, this time summoning all the moisture in the air, the dew from any nearby trees, the water from a small stream not too far from where they stood. A bubble of water formed and zoomed straight toward Luke.

Still laughing, Luke shouted, "Oh, shit!" And he tried to dive and roll around the rolling earth, but it was no use. Kara laughed as hard as she could when she saw the bubble of water drop like a bomb on Luke.

The earth stopped rolling and Luke stood, drenched from head to toe.

Shane and Kara doubled over laughing, and Luke stood there, dripping with a scowl on his face. But he only watched them for a few seconds before he was laughing too. He couldn't stay mad. He knew he must have been a sight.

"Next time, let's bring squirt guns!" Luke shouted into the night, Kara far behind him and Shane far in front of him.

Still laughing, Kara responded. "No, you'll be bringing ammo for him to the fight! We need to come up with a better way to get him."

"Oh, I'll get him, that little shit," Luke turned back to Shane and crouched to run at him, when the sound of a gun being cocked stopped him where he stood.

A man in a bathrobe, middle-aged and beer-bellied, stood with a gun aimed at Shane. "Are you the ones who've been killing my livestock?" he shouted at Shane, and, boy!, was he angry.

Shane looked at Luke, confusion plastered all across his face. This guy thought they were there to kill his livestock?

Shane took a step toward the man, his hands up in surrender. "Sir, it's all a complete misunderstanding.

We had no idea we were on your property. We'll leave now."

"Don't come any closer. I'll shoot!" The man's voice was steady, but his hands shook.

"It's fine. We're leaving." Shane stopped walking, but he didn't retreat either. Luke, dripping wet and still smirking, headed toward Shane. Shane watched the man's eyes dart toward Luke's movement.

But it was Kara who caught the man by surprise.

Like a flash of lightning, she darted in from off in the distance. The man probably hadn't known she was there. And, other than looking like she'd just resurrected from the dead, he probably wouldn't have considered her a threat if he'd seen her anyway. Little did this man know that she was the most aggressive of the three.

She tackled the man and sank her fangs deep into his throat, swallowing big pulls of his blood. The force from Kara triggered the shotgun and the bullet whizzed toward Shane's head. He deflected the bullet easily with a gust of air and it flew off into the distance, landing somewhere down the hill. Shane used his power to yank the gun from the man's hands and tossed it off to the side.

Meanwhile, Luke ran at vampire speed to Kara. He wrapped his arms around her midsection and yanked her off the man. "You don't have to kill him, remember?"

Kara let Luke pull her off the unconscious man, her mouth dripping with sticky, red, coppery blood. Luke helped her back to her feet and she stood there staring at the half-dead man. Shane wondered what she was thinking, but he guessed that it probably had something to do with wanting to finish him off.

He watched her in the moonlight, her hair disheveled and dirty. Her mouth and the front of her shirt were covered in blood. Her fangs were still extended and dripping. She was a mess.

Shane summoned more water and dropped the bubble on her, splashing Luke—again—and the man she'd accosted, but drenching Kara from head to toe. Kara was not amused.

"What? You needed a shower," Shane said with a smile.

Luke laughed at that, and soon Kara was laughing too. And they all stood there laughing, some still dripping, standing over a half-dead middle-aged man.

After a minute, Kara looked down at the man she'd almost killed and then back to Shane. "Can we go home now?"

It warmed Shane's heart that she'd called the compound home. She was really taking to this life so much better than he had.

Luke put an arm around Kara's soaking shoulders and led her toward Shane. Shane reached out a hand and took hers in his. Suddenly, she was like a little sister to him and again he thought of Julianna.

His heart ached at the loss.

"Yeah, let's go home, Kara," Shane said with what he hoped was a warm smile.

"What do we do with this guy?' Luke asked, shoving the man with his foot.

Shane shrugged. "Not much we can do. He's his wife's problem now. We have our own." Luke shrugged in response. He didn't really care that much.

Back at the compound, Shane took Kara up to the third floor and showed her the room he wanted her to have. It was painted a soft cream color, with a lace covering on the bed. He didn't know who had decorated this room before him, but considering its classic style, he assumed it was an older vampire.

There was a small lamp on a bedside table and a rocking chair in the corner. But Kara had bolted straight to the double doors which led to a balcony. She opened the doors and stepped out into the night air. A thousand lights twinkled before her. From up here, you could see a lot of the Valley.

"Isabelle can take you to get clothes tomorrow night, but for now you can look through the dresser in here and borrow whatever you need to," Shane explained. "There's a shower down the hall if you want to properly clean up after our night on the town."

Kara turned and smiled at Shane. "Thanks. This

room is great. The view... is beautiful. Kind of reminds me of my dad's house in Ventura."

"I grew up on the other side of this hill," Shane explained. Compared to older vampires, they'd grown up practically in the same backyard.

"How old are you?" Kara asked, her head cocked to the side, her hair still an unruly mess.

Shane crossed his arms against his chest, a night breeze blowing past them on the balcony and tousling his blonde curls. "I'm not much older than you. It's barely been more than a week since I resurrected myself."

"Not as a vampire. As Shane. How old are you?" Kara asked again.

"Twenty," Shane answered simply.

Kara frowned a bit and then grabbed both Shane's hands and squeezed them. "That's very young. It won't be easy."

Shane was confused. "What won't be easy?"

"Is she a vampire too?" Kara still looked haunted.

Shane shook his head, still holding hands with Kara. "Who are we talking about?"

"My stepmother. Theresa."

"Oh." Shane's shoulders fell. He hated to be the one who had to break the news to her. "No. Theresa's a witch." He squeezed Kara's hands. "She hates vampires. I'm afraid she's your enemy now."

"She's always been my enemy." Kara's eyes turned dark, her scowl deepening. "I don't know how she did it, but I'm sure she murdered my mother."

Shane didn't know what to say to that. He figured that Kara was probably right. Theresa *had* probably murdered her mother. He wouldn't put it past her. Kara walked back into her new bedroom and sat on the bed.

"Well, I hope we win." She smiled up at him.

"We will." Shane said with the certainty he felt. "And I understand if you're not ready for the fight."

"Oh, I'm ready." Kara smiled maliciously. With her dirty, ratted hair she looked like the frightening vampire she was. "I was ready to kill her before I became a vampire. Now? I'll rip her head from her body and drink her blood slowly."

And Shane knew she could do it, too.

4

On his way downstairs from Kara's bedroom, Shane peeked into what was now Camilla's room to check on her. She was able to stay up late to be on the vampire schedule, but usually by early morning, she couldn't take it anymore and fell asleep.

He was surprised when he cracked the door open to see her sitting up on the bed looking back at him.

"Sorry to disturb you," Shane whispered and started to close the door.

"Don't be. I was waiting for you to come home." Camilla patted the bed next to her, encouraging him to come join her. She was a vision even in a t-shirt and sweats. Her hair was tight in a side ponytail that rested on her shoulder. Shane noticed she often liked to wear it that way: with her hair over one shoulder. He could smell her from the doorway and the urge to reach out and touch her hair almost overcame him.

As he crossed the room to sit on her bed, she grabbed his hand and pulled him toward her. "How did Kara do?" Her breath was soft and warm. So close to his. Shane watched her lips and tried to focus on her words and not on wanting to kiss her. It would be as easy as leaning forward an inch and their lips would touch.

He licked his lips nervously. "Um, she did great, actually. I tried to be a good teacher and quickly realized I was wasting my time. It's completely natural for her." He sat on the bed next to Camilla, leaning back against the bed frame. He thought maybe a little distance would dampen his desire to touch her hair and face.

It didn't.

Camilla did nothing to help him when she scooted closer and rested her head on his shoulder, one hand toying with her ponytail. He pulled her tighter up against his side and held her close.

"Theresa wanted her to become a witch. I wonder if Kara knew that?" Camilla wondered aloud. "I wonder what she'll do now that her two favorites are sleeping in your house."

"You were a favorite too?" Shane asked, tilting his head down toward the beauty at his side.

Camilla nodded. "I was her protégé. She wanted to train me to be the next Coven leader. But Elyse clearly wanted and deserves that position. I haven't even regenerated once yet."

"Is that how witches remain immortal like vampires? By regenerating?" Shane asked.

Camilla sat up on her knees and turned toward Shane. "Yes. We basically cheat death. It's a potion similar to the one she gave your betrayer." Shane hissed softly at the mention of Dimas, Julianna's murderer. "It regenerates you, keeps you young and if you get mortally wounded or ill, your body just heals itself. Witches have to do this every twenty-five years or so, so they don't age."

"But what would she tell her family? When she still looked twenty-nine when she was supposed to be sixty?"

Camilla snorted. "No way will her family still be alive the next time Theresa regenerates. After what happened to Kara, I wouldn't be surprised if Emily and Richard are already dead."

Shane frowned at that. He knew he'd done what needed to be done. He couldn't be a wallflower in the games of witches and vampires, but he'd never meant for a young girl to be killed in the process.

Camilla looked down at the bedding beneath her, as if she were unable to meet Shane's eyes. He gently placed a finger on her chin and pulled her face upward so she was looking at him again. She watched him carefully for a moment, smiling slightly at his handsome face and stunning blue eyes.

"They have to kill children," she stated softly. Shane wrinkled his brow in confusion, so she clarified. "To regenerate. Witches need the blood of children."

Camilla grabbed his hands and squeezed them gently. "You see? You think vampires are monsters. But witches are monsters too."

She looked away again and whispered, "I'm a monster, too."

Shane scooted closer to her and cupped her face with both hands. "In a million years, you could never be a monster. Just like me, you've done things you regret. But you did what you had to do to survive. That makes you a survivor." He looked deep into her brown eyes, the color of milk chocolate. Every curve of her face was perfection. Her nose was just the right angle, with a slight turn-up at the end. Her full lips parted and she let out a small breath.

And as he watched her face closely, amazed by her beauty, she quickly moved toward him, closing the gap and pressing her lips to his. He was taken by surprise but did nothing to stop her. In fact, he deepened the kiss, moving one hand to her hip and pulling her even closer to him. She wrapped her arms around him and pressed her chest to his.

And then she surprised him again by climbing on his lap, straddling him. She grabbed his neck and pulled him closer still, as she darted her tongue inside his slightly parted lips. Shane moved his hands to her back, rubbing up and under her T-shirt. Her skin was soft and warm and responded positively to his touch. He was just about to flip her on her back when she broke the kiss and pulled away.

Her breathing was heavier than a moment ago and she had a huge smile on her lips. Shane was wearing a matching smile, only he was positive his expression looked ridiculous compared to her seductiveness.

She licked her lips and then said, "I have a present for you."

Intrigued, he asked, "Do you?"

She hopped off his lap and reached over toward her nightstand. Shane watched her and fought the urge to grab her again and continue where they had left off. When she pulled back from the nightstand, she had a small black velvet bag in her hand. Shane was disappointed to see she stayed seated on the bed and not back on his lap where he wanted her, but her smile warmed his heart. She was clearly proud of the present.

"Hold out your hand," Camilla instructed.

Shane did as he was told, holding his hand out, palm up, in front of Camilla. Still grinning, she plopped the bag into Shane's hand.

"Is this a hex bag?" Shane asked, not entirely sure what the gift meant.

"Yes. To use against your enemies," Camilla stated, still smiling.

Shane had found when he cleared his emotions and thoughts, he could sense truths easily. "This is for me to use against Theresa?"

Camilla nodded. "If you use this, she won't be able to hurt you ever again."

Shane studied Camilla's smiling face once more. Not since Julianna had he had someone who protected him like this. "You made this? For me?"

Camilla nodded again. "I know you're powerful. I've seen what you can do and it's breathtaking. But,"

Camilla looked sheepish again, "Theresa is powerful too. And she's been at it for centuries."

To Shane, Camilla was a jumble of intoxicating paradoxes. At once she was strong, yet shy. Exotic, yet simple. Protective, yet herself vulnerable.

"I love that you want to protect me," Shane said, grinning a half-smile.

She rubbed his cheek with her hand, so tenderly and gently. Her eyes were adoring. Could he sense Camilla reflecting back the same feelings he felt?

She spoke softly, her voice like a caress. "I'll always protect you, Shane."

Camilla leaned in again, but this time slowly. Shane met her halfway, moving slowly as well. Their lips met again, but the kiss was tender, loving. When they parted, Shane rested his forehead against hers, and cupped the back of her neck.

"I want to go with you," Camilla stated.

Shane pulled back. "Where?"

"Wherever it was you were planning to go after you checked in on me." Camilla smiled. "I know you can walk in the sun. And I know something was on your mind."

Shane huffed. "Am I that easy to read?"

Camilla shook her head. "Only to someone who watches your every move, wanting to know everything about you. I know you have a good heart." She reached up and moved a blond curl back into place on the top of his head. "And I know something has been on your mind. I don't know what."

Shane sat up straight and thought about it. He had only known Camilla a few days. Was he really ready for this?

"Okay. You can come with me." Shane stood, reaching out a hand to help Camilla off the bed. "If you truly want to know everything about me, then this would definitely be the best way to start."

Camilla wrapped her arms around his waist. Looking up at him, she said, "Where are we going?"

"To my childhood home." Shane then grabbed Camilla's hand and pulled her along with him.

When they stepped out the front door of the

compound, the bright morning sun blinded Shane. Yes, he could tolerate the daylight, but he still rarely went out during the day. He was a nocturnal creature now, and rarely was there a chance or reason to do much during the day. He felt its warmth and waited until his eyes adjusted to the brightness. In the distance, he heard a bird chirping. The ground was covered in a layer of dew. He'd forgotten how beautiful the morning could be.

He took a moment to smell the fresh air. This wasn't exactly the beachfront property of Regina's former Bellinz compound, but he was fairly certain he could even smell the salty ocean air. It was going to be a beautiful day, and he was truly thankful that he was the rare vampire who could enjoy it.

"It's probably best if you hop on my back. We can get there faster that way." Shane helped Camilla into essentially a piggyback ride. "Hold on tight."

With her arms wrapped comfortably around Shane's neck, her body pressed against his strong back, Camilla enjoyed the ride. His vampire speed made it feel like she was flying, the wind whipping past her face and blowing back her hair. She watched as they ascended the mountain and entered the valley on the other side.

The community Shane headed toward was anything but flashy. The houses were one-story ranches, slightly on the rundown side. Some had freshly cut, well-kept lawns while others were overgrown fields with cars rusting in the middle of the front yards.

Shane slowed as he approached a cute, white house with sky blue trim. The front of the house was accented with red brick. It wasn't exuding wealth, but it was neat and clean. And happy. Camilla sensed the kind of happy home she would have wanted. Two loving parents, two kids and a dog. It was like waving a fairy wand and suddenly you had the perfect all-American family. And it warmed her heart to know he'd come from humble roots.

There was a large tree out front, and Shane stopped beneath it, one hand on the trunk. Camilla slid slowly off his back but kept one hand on him in solidarity. He was watching the house pensively and she wondered what he was thinking. Did he miss this life? Or was he happy it was over?

"This is where you lived before you...um." She cleared her throat, thinking of the right way to say it. "Before you resurrected."

Shane's eyebrows were crossed and his face was dark, but she knew he wasn't directing any negative emotion toward her. "You can say it. Before I died." He turned to her, gently touching her ponytail. "And yes, this is where I lived when I was human."

Camilla didn't know what you were supposed to say in these types of situations, so she said nothing.

After a moment, he looked into her eyes. "I wonder how things might have been different if you and I had met before I was a vampire and you were a witch."

She grabbed his hand and held it lovingly in her own. "There's no reason to spend a moment thinking about that. Our paths would never have crossed if we'd stayed in those lives." Camilla stepped closer. "And I love who you are."

Camilla had a loose tendril of brown hair and

Shane gently tucked it behind her ear. "You know I had sister, right?"

She nodded. She knew more than she wished she knew. "She was killed by the betrayer, right? I heard the stories." Her voice was soft, caring.

Shane squinted in the sunlight as he stared at his childhood home. For a moment it seemed he was lost in thought, reliving some old memory from way back when. "And did you know she was the one who turned me?"

Camilla rested a hand on Shane's shoulder. "It must've been hard to lose her. I'm so sorry, Shane."

Shane was quiet for a moment, so Camilla just watched him silently, giving him the time to think. She knew it must be hard, everyone expecting so much from you. And he was just a young man. Handsome and caring.

There was a bird singing in a nearby tree. Crickets chirped in a sing-song way. There were cars leaving for work, so the occasional voice of people starting their day broke through the sounds of nature.

But overall, the morning was peaceful. Camilla enjoyed having a day that wasn't filled with plotting, scheming, and backstabbing. *Ah, the life of a witch!*

Shane listened hard for sounds inside the home he had grown up in. There was only silence echoing within its walls. And both cars were gone from the driveway. "Come on." Shane pulled Camilla's hand gently. "I want to show you something."

He walked purposefully around to the side gate. His head was held high, like breaking into someone's property were no big deal. Camilla, on the other hand, felt deceitful. She wondered what Shane's parents would do if they came face-to-face with their dead son. Shane led Camilla along a skinny side yard where they stepped into a small, but cute backyard. The grass was neatly cut, rose bushes nicely trimmed. Either Shane's parents had green thumbs, or they had a really good gardener.

On a covered patio, there was a porch swing and a nice little patio set with green-striped cushions. Shane took a very brief look around and then walked straight to the mat by the sliding glass door.

"Does it feel weird being here?" Camilla asked, as she watched Shane expertly break into his parents' home.

From where he was crouched down low retrieving the key that was hidden under the mat, Shane looked up and over his shoulder. "Not really. A couple weeks ago, I still lived here."

He pulled the key out and walked over to a door to the right of the patio. With a twist and a pop, the door unlocked and opened to a dark garage. Shane entered and Camilla followed. It was musty and reminded Camilla of an old attic. Boxes and tools, and old furniture were stacked every which way and covered in layers of dust. Clearly, the Walker family used their garage for storage.

Weaving in and out of all the items piled around them, Shane led Camilla to another door further inside the garage. He tried the handle, and it opened with ease.

"They never lock this door," Shane explained.

They stepped into a bright, cheery kitchen.

Sunlight was streaming in through the front window and bouncing off the white countertops. The walls were a happy soft yellow color. The kitchen furniture was white and bright, and everything made Camilla feel warm and happy.

"Your mom has a bubbly personality, doesn't she?" Camilla asked.

Shane nodded. "Yes. Julianna takes so much after her." Then he caught himself. "Took so much after her."

Shane reached for Camilla's hand again and led her through a living room with a small couch, coffee table and television set. They walked down a short hall and at the end of the hall was a bathroom. But Shane turned right, stopping before a closed door.

He put his hand on the door handle, but he didn't open it right away. "This is my room."

Camilla watched in silence. She didn't want to rush him, didn't even want to go in if it made him uncomfortable. Although a small part of her was curious to see where the young, human Shane Walker had once lived a peaceful, and maybe even happy, life. Before he was "the chosen one" from the Dark Prophecy, he was just a kid with shaggy blonde hair who liked to hang out with friends and go to the beach.

With a twist of his wrist, he opened the door. He gestured for Camilla to go first, but then he followed immediately behind her. Camilla honestly hadn't fully expected him to. And she hadn't really known what to expect when she saw his room, but somehow it suited him perfectly. It reminded her that beyond being the uniter and leader of vampires, he was just a kid who was torn from his life against his will. Not all that dissimilarly from the way she had been. They were both victims in a sense.

She turned a full circle. The walls were painted a neutral tan color, with furniture and bedspread accenting the room in black. The far wall had a built-in bookshelf next to a mirrored sliding closet door. The walls each had a poster to decorate the room. Over the bed was a large poster of a man on a surfboard. In block print it said "Laird Hamilton," and then a squiggly signature filled out the corner. Camilla didn't know who Laird Hamilton was, but she assumed he was some kind of popular surfer. A concert poster for Coldplay hung on the wall behind where Shane was now leaning, his arms folded. Everything was neat and clean, as if his mom still came in here once a week to dust and smooth the creases out of the bed she'd made, even though it hadn't been slept in since Shane died.

"I didn't come back here to see my room, but I thought you might like to," Shane said with a shrug, trying to cover up his emotions but doing a terrible job of it. Camilla could tell a part of him just wanted to come home.

"Thank you for sharing this with me." She walked over to Shane and wrapped her arms around his waist, her head on his chest. He put one arm around her shoulder, but otherwise he tried to remain stoic. She wasn't buying it, but she wasn't going to push it either. After a moment, Camilla looked up at Shane and asked, "What did we come here for then?"

Shane jerked his head toward the doorway. "It's

in Julianna's old room."

Camilla pulled back from embracing Shane but waited for him to lead the way down the hall. She closed the door to Shane's old room with a final peek inside. Past the bathroom on the left was another room. Shane opened the door to a room that clearly belonged to a teenage girl. There was a chair rail around the room with the top half painted a soft lavender and the bottom half white. The bed had a floral print. More posters adorned the walls, and over a dressing mirror hung dozens of pictures of girls at football games, formal dances, riding around in cars, at sleepovers. Camilla had never really had many freedoms before she'd joined up with Theresa, but she imagined that Julianna must have had a carefree life.

In contrast, Camilla's parents had been domineering. Controlling.

"Julianna's room," Shane announced.

"I figured," Camilla smirked. Picking up one of the pictures on the dressing table, Camilla told Shane, "I never went to a high school dance. My parents thought it was improper."

Shane lifted the bed skirt up and began peering under. "So they drove you to witchcraft instead. Really strategic."

Camilla looked around the room, swallowing the jealousy that was building. "You don't know how lucky you were, Shane. You guys had a beautiful family."

He stopped rummaging under Julianna's old bed and looked up at Camilla. Her eyes were sad, heavy with the weight of wasted years. He answered her, "I do know. I almost wish my parents had been dicks. It would make it a lot easier to live a second life as a vampire and forget what I've had taken away. And what's been taken from them."

Camilla nodded. She could understand that. In all her regrets of succumbing to Theresa's persuasion, she never once regretted leaving home or missed her childhood in the least, even though she'd always known how much her parents loved her.

Shane dug around again for a few moments and then held up a notebook. "Aha! Found it."

It looked so plain and unassuming. Camilla couldn't imagine what he would want a notebook so badly for. "What is it?"

"Julianna's diary." Shane stood back up. "From when she was human. I used to read it all the time when she died, or when she was turned. But I didn't know she was a vampire back then. I'd watched her be buried, and that was it."

Camilla fought the urge to hug him yet again. How hard it must have been to lose someone you love *twice*. Instead, she squeezed his hand. Suddenly, she saw his eyes go wide, complete shock lining his face. "What?"

"My mom. I hear her voice." Shane's voice was barely above a whisper, so frozen was he by the worry she might see him, combined with the pain of hearing her voice again—a sound he'd never expected to have the comfort of hearing with vampire ears. "What's she doing home? She should be at work."

Camilla knew his hearing was really heightened. "How far away does she sound?"

"She's in the driveway, talking to a neighbor," Shane explained, bolting out of Julianna's room and heading straight to his old room. He had a large window out front where he could see up and down the whole street. "Shit!"

"She'll be traumatized more than you if she sees you, Shane. We've got to get out of here. Now." Camilla urged Shane from the doorway of his room.

Shane nodded but didn't move for a few seconds. He stood, staring at his mom from his old bedroom window. His forehead was creased and he sat lost in thought. Camilla wished she could give him more time, but she knew there'd be no way to explain this.

"Shane," she urged again gently.

"Yeah." Shane pulled away from the window, swallowing the emotion of seeing his mother and grabbing Camilla's hand as he walked past, closing the door behind him. He pulled Camilla back down the hallway and back through the living room. They were there in the middle of the room when he heard keys jiggling in a lock. His mom was opening the front door.

Silently, Shane and Camilla exchanged a worried glance. Shane could use vampire super speed, but Camilla couldn't. They ran to the kitchen, trying to step as lightly as they could, and hid crouched down below the countertop. If Mrs. Walker decided to go straight to the kitchen, there'd be no way to avoid being seen.

The front door opened with a stream of light encasing Shane's mother. He couldn't resist the desire to lift his head above the counter to catch a glimpse. Camilla yanked him down. Her heart was hammering in her chest. She didn't want to witness the scene if Mrs. Walker saw her dead son crouching in her kitchen. The best-case scenario is that she'd simply pass out from shock.

Mrs. Walker entered the living room and walked quickly toward the kitchen. Camilla and Shane froze as they heard her approaching footsteps. But as suddenly as she'd appeared, she stopped walking, turned on her heels and walked down the hall in the opposite direction, humming a tune as she went.

Camilla exhaled a heavy sigh and Shane took the

opportunity to bolt for the kitchen door back out to the garage. They ran so fast they didn't take the time to shut anything gently, and Mrs. Walker could have sworn she heard a door slam.

On her way back to her car, she investigated half-heartedly and didn't see anything out of place, so she wrote it all off to the wind. She had no idea her undead baby boy had just been there moments ago.

Back at the formerly Strashni compound, Shane walked Camilla to her room across from his and bid her good rest. He was exhausted. Camilla had so many questions to ask him about the notebook and his family, but she decided to just stick with the warning that had been nagging her the past few days.

"I think you should plan something offensive against Theresa," Camilla blurted to Shane before he could leave her doorway.

"Where is this coming from?" Shane leaned against the door jamb.

"I know Theresa. She'll be plotting something. We've been focusing on Kara, and I support that completely, but I don't want to be caught unaware. Theresa *will* be hellbent on revenge."

Shane smirked. He loved that she was worried, but he'd been thinking the same thing. "You're absolutely right. And I owe both Theresa and Dimas a little revenge of my own."

He kissed Camilla softly one last time and headed into his own room just across the hallway.

5

Emily felt her pulse quicken at the prospect of her first official act as a witch to be raising someone from the dead.

She already felt the memory of her old life fading into the distance. The power, the magic, the sisterhood of the coven. All things she hadn't known she'd been needing in her life.

How stupid cheerleading suddenly seemed. How stupid high school now seemed. All pointless. She'd been living the life of a useless zombie and had been completely ignorant.

Sunlight was beginning to stream into the warehouse through the high windows which lined the top of the walls, close to the ceiling. The daylight served as a spotlight on the ceremony before her. She could see specks of dust floating all around inside the light, cascading down around them as they stood in the center of the warehouse.

The witches of Harbor Coven stood in a circle around the now-uncovered body of the dead vampire, Julianna Walker. She was lying on a table, her severed head less than half an inch from her cold, white corpse. Emily couldn't believe they had the power to bring this vampire back to life. And Theresa would have the power to control her. Julianna would be like a living doll. Emily smiled wickedly at the thought.

Don't worry, Kara. We'll avenge you.

Emily held the basket as she'd been instructed, as Theresa pulled out bay leaves and twigs of rosemary and lined them all around the body. Emily was so honored to have been asked to assist. As a new witch, she figured Elyse or someone would be chosen ahead of her, so she held her head high as she followed Theresa around the corpse.

When the body was properly outlined, Theresa

walked over to the work bench where she stored all her potion-making ingredients. Emily watched carefully and took mental notes, eager to learn everything Theresa could teach her. She grabbed spices, animal body parts, including what looked like a rat's tail, and then a few of the hairs Theresa had pulled from Julianna's severed head. When she was satisfied with the ingredients, she mashed them with a stone until they were blended in a goopy mixture that looked to Emily like a distorted version of clay.

Theresa turned toward the circle of witches, and Emily did the same. Theresa held the bowl with the mashed ingredients high above her head.

"Blood is the main ingredient for life. And we have all agreed to pay the price," Theresa instructed, her voice powerful and booming and leaving absolutely no room for argument. "I will pass the bowl and the knife around the circle. Each of you will open a vein and let your life force mix with the potion."

Emily watched in horror as Theresa took the knife to her wrist and sliced willingly across the meaty flesh, cutting open her wrist as if there were no pain involved at all. Without thinking, Emily covered her mouth and her eyes welled with tears. For a moment, she was just a sixteen-year-old girl again, feeling small and helpless amongst powerful creatures. Theresa let what Emily thought was quite a bit of blood pour from her wrist into the mixture, and then she turned to Emily with the bowl and the knife.

When Theresa saw Emily looking scared, she had to cool her anger. Emily had come so far today, and then suddenly she was back to being a big baby. With a soft, but tight and controlled tone, Theresa leaned into Emily. "You said you wanted to be a witch. Suck it up and prove it."

With a stern face, Theresa handed the bowl and the knife to Emily. Emily swallowed hard and accepted the items. She knew Theresa was right, and because of the protection potion no harm would come to her, but it didn't make the prospect of taking a knife to her body any more palatable. Emily steeled herself and forced herself to think of Kara fighting for her life beneath a vampire's fangs. If Kara could endure that, Emily could take a little cut. With a swift movement, acting before she could overthink it, Emily sliced her wrist and aimed her bloody wrist over the bowl.

Emily smiled. It had hurt a little, but she could already feel the healing powers taking over and the pain easing. She walked to the closest witch and laid the bowl on the floor beneath her, handing her the knife. One by one, the witches sliced and dripped into the ingredients. By the tenth witch, the potion was smoking like the powerful spell it was.

When they had all taken their turns, Theresa struck a match and dropped it into the bowl. The witches all watched as it burst into a fireball, a few feet high. Then it slowly burnt itself back out, leaving a pile of ash in the bowl.

"Get in position, witches," Theresa instructed, as she lifted the bowl and walked toward the corpse.

The witches quickly formed a circle again around the body. They all seemed to have a designated place. Emily saw a small hole she assumed was formerly Camilla's position and took it. No one argued, so she assumed this would be her new place. As the witches got into position, Theresa shook the bowl over the body, letting ash rain down on Julianna's body from severed head to lifeless foot. When Theresa was done, she placed the bowl on the floor, and Julianna was buried under a thin layer of what looked as innocuous as Cinderella's ashes.

Standing over the body, Theresa shouted the words of the spell, her arms raised to the sky like she was calling on a higher power. Perhaps she was, but Emily wondered if maybe she was reaching in the wrong direction. "Gehennam ignis superextendam in artus!"

The second time around, all the witches joined in, copying Theresa with their arms raised in the air. Many of them were also swaying as if there was a hymn playing that only they could hear. "Gehennam ignis superextendam in artus!"

They repeated the spell over and over, getting louder and louder as they did, heading for a witchcraft crescendo.

Little did they know, hidden in the shadows behind a pile of boxes where the sunlight couldn't reach him, a vampire with stringy white hair stood watching and grinning like a crocodile. Patience. It was always about patience. What did Shane or anyone less than a century old truly know about biding their time and waiting for the right moment to strike.

He allowed himself to be excited about Julianna's rebirth. Yes, he had been honest that he thought she would be a great pawn in the witches' plot for revenge, but there had been a piece he had purposefully left out of the narrative. He truly cared for Julianna. She had always been loyal to him and had looked at him with tenderness and reverence. No one else had ever looked at him the way Julianna did. Soon she would arise and re-awaken his heart.

He watched the witches, repeating their spell with their arms in the air, listened as they got louder and louder with their chant. "Gehennam ignis superextendam in artus!"

He giggled with the anticipation, mixed with his own feelings of malice and revenge. And then there was another burst of flame. It was short and loud, like a quick explosion and Dimas panicked. Had something gone wrong? From his vantage point, he couldn't see details, just heard the murmuring of the witches in the circle.

But Emily could see just fine.

She watched as the neck of the sister of her sworn enemy stitched itself back together. A light, like a blue flame, flickered around her neck as the magic worked to undo what had been done. Once the neck was sewn back together, flesh re-attached to flesh, Emily watched the flame dance itself from Julianna's head all the way down to her toes.

And then the murmuring stopped. An eerie silence filled the room as everyone waited to see if the spell had worked. Even Dimas had to peek his head out from behind the boxes. There was nothing moving, no sounds of cars or nature in the distance, just a total hush.

And then Julianna's right foot twitched. One of the witches gasped and Theresa glared at her. They continued watching in silence as Julianna's other foot twitched. And then her knees began to shake. Emily had no idea if this was what was *supposed* to happen, but it didn't feel right. It looked like a bad allergic reaction, the way her bottom half of her body convulsed on the table.

"Come join us, Betrayer. I know you're here," Theresa shouted toward the boxes where Dimas was watching and waiting.

He stepped out from behind the boxes but stayed close to them as he slithered his way over to the witches' circle. One foot forward and he would step into the sunlight and scorch his almost translucent white skin. Theresa laughed at him.

Theresa watched Julianna with pure pride. In all her centuries on the earth, she had never raised anyone from the dead. Quite the contrary. Mostly she was killing people who stood in her way or who could help her in her quest for power and money. Seeing Shane's sister's dead body alive with movement was a crowning achievement. Now she just had to make extra sure she could control this puppet, or things could go very wrong. She needed to stay in control. She hated when she wasn't in control.

And she had to get a moment to kill Dimas, but that was a plan for another day.

As suddenly as the convulsing started, it stopped. Everyone took a step forward. Even Dimas—who then had to jump back as his flesh began to sizzle in the streaming sunlight. Julianna lay there still, her neck attached to her body with a ridged scar. For a second, seeds of doubt began to creep into their minds. Had the spell not worked?

But then Julianna sat up with a jerk. A few witches stepped back and gasped. Not Emily. She stepped even closer. This was her first official spell as a witch and it was a big one. She couldn't believe that a once-dead body was now sitting up on the table in front of her.

At the sight of Julianna's confused, terrified

eyes, Theresa stepped into mother-mode, the one she'd honed the past few years stepmothering Richard's children and playing house. She wasn't really concerned about Julianna's state of mind. She wanted to make sure she controlled the situation.

Theresa sat on the table next to Julianna and smoothed her ratty blonde curls with one hand. She spoke in a cooing voice. "There, there now. You're okay. You're among your new family." She tucked Julianna under her arm and held her close. Julianna still looked like an animal caught in a rat trap. The slightest sound could have made her run at vampire speed. Everyone in the room held their breath. Theresa continued, "Tell me, what do you remember?"

Julianna turned frightened eyes toward Theresa and licked her lips. "Uhhhh," the wheels in her just-revitalized brain began to turn. "Luke. I remember Luke."

"Shit," Dimas tried to mutter from the shadows, but everyone heard him. A few heads even turned.

But Julianna continued, speaking aloud what

her brain was trying to pull back together. "He was mad. He was angry."

Theresa soothed Julianna, rubbing her shoulders with a gentleness that was barely recognizable. "Yes. Luke was angry. Do you remember that he was the one who killed you?"

Julianna's eyes grew large at the information. "Luke killed me?"

"Yes." Theresa continued to soothe her and rub her shoulders. "Luke killed you, and your brother did nothing."

"My brother?" Julianna's forehead creased with thought, almost like it was too overwhelming for her. "Shane?"

"Yes, Shane. You remember." Theresa smiled and then gently kissed Julianna's forehead. "But don't worry. We've healed you and we'll be your new family. You're one of us now."

Dimas watched Theresa work and admired her from the shadows. She was a master at deception and Dimas felt like he was watching an artist create a masterpiece. Julianna was accepting every falsehood Theresa fed her.

"Why would Luke kill me?" Julianna asked, her voice small and sad.

"Because you knew too much." Dimas didn't know if Theresa had prepared all these words, or if she was winging it, but the lies just slipped off her tongue with barely an effort. "After everything you did for Luke and Shane, they betrayed you in their lust for power."

"They betrayed me," Julianna whispered.

"But you are safe now. We'll protect you," Theresa explained, continuing to hug Julianna and ensure her false sense of security before they used her to exact their revenge.

Dimas could barely take it anymore, the longing to be the one comforting Julianna. From the shadows where he hid, he almost shouted, "Julianna."

Julianna's face lit up with recognition. A face she knew and trusted. "Lord Dimas! I'm so glad to see you!" She held her arms out to him, encouraging him to come to her for an embrace.

"You'll have to come to me, Julianna. I can't step into the sunlight," Dimas explained.

And then Emily and Theresa exchanged a glance.

Elyse was the one to state what they hadn't even been paying attention to the whole time Theresa had been brainwashing Julianna. "She's not a vampire anymore. Julianna's human!"

For a moment, confusion filled Julianna's face again. "Vampire?" A thousand thoughts swirled in her brain as she remembered her five years of drinking blood and fulfilling prophecies. It was a murky memory, the kind you have to dig deep for and then only remember bits and pieces of. But it had been true. She remembered being a vampire. Julianna tried to extend her fangs and claws, but nothing came. She felt her teeth and they were as normal as they had been before she'd died. Looking up at Elyse, the reality was painted across her face. "She's right. I'm human."

Emily let a smile creep across her face. This day had been a complete miracle. Kara wasn't doomed to be a vampire—they now knew the cure. She could have her sister back, just as she'd always been.

Theresa jumped off the table, her eyes locked on Emily. But where Emily let her emotions and thoughts dance wildly across her face, Theresa remained a stoic mask. Plots and deception were games that had to be kept to yourself at all times. She would need to teach her young protégé that. "Well, isn't this an interesting turn of events?"

Elyse looked to the leader of the Harbor Coven. "So what do we do now, Theresa?"

Theresa grabbed Julianna's hand and helped her climb off the table and into the circle with the other witches. The witches even expanded their circle so Dimas could join in from where he stood by the boxes.

Dimas and Julianna both looked confused and uneasy, but they said nothing.

"Witches," Theresa announced. "It's time to set our new plan into motion. We must help Julianna get revenge on her murderers." Theresa's eyes narrowed, even as Julianna looked uncomfortable at the news.

"And tonight we go get my daughter back."

Her slight nod to Emily was the only indication that she was thinking the same thing as her young stepdaughter. They would get Kara, kill her and return her to her human life.

6

Elias was the first to join Shane, Luke and Camilla. He stepped into the basement of Shane's compound and clutched Shane's shoulder in a brotherly greeting. He then shook Luke's hand and nodded in greeting to the young witch. He liked Camilla but was afraid to touch her.

Centuries of habits died hard.

The sun had set a few hours ago, so the basement was lined with the soft light of a handful of lamps. A Vampire Council had no need for strong lighting. Other than Camilla they could all see as well in the dark as they could with the lights on. Shane had set up multiple couches and seating for all the various vampire leaders. Back when Dimas ran this compound there had been virtually nowhere to sit. Shane tried not to look where his sister had been murdered a short while ago. None of the Vampire Council knew the details, and he wanted to keep it that way.

Elias stood by Luke, ever the bodyguard. Even though now he was one of the leaders on the council, he couldn't shake centuries of being a warrior. He was tall, and fierce, with long black hair and a warrior's body and soul.

And Shane was happy to have him by his side. He liked and trusted Elias.

Isabelle came in shortly after Elias, with Damian at her side. He had been her leader in the Fortis tribe, and even though he had never been a great leader and the Fortis tribe no longer existed, Isabelle felt like Damian was family. She'd been waiting at the front door to greet him and escort him down to the council meeting. And on this council he had no power over her.

"Damian, glad you could join us," Shane said as he shook Damian's hand.

Damian said nothing, couldn't even look Shane

in the eye, but nodded in acknowledgement. Shane's power was overwhelming to some.

Regina walked in with Alexi at her side. It went unsaid, but the conclusion everyone jumped to was that Alexi had taken Marcus' place as Regina's second in command and plaything in bed. She was as beautiful as ever, with her thick full lips painted red and her long black hair falling down her back. She sauntered toward Shane as if she knew how beautiful she was.

Camilla watched Regina carefully as she approached Shane. Camilla held her breath as Regina put her arms around him and pulled his head to her chest, forcing him against her full bosom. Isabelle just laughed.

She offered no words of greeting, just rocked him in her arms with his head to her chest. "You know you can always talk to Regina if you need to," Regina said, annoying Camilla like crazy when she spoke of herself in the third person. Alexi looked on, almost bored.

When she finally released Shane, he looked

straight at Camilla and shrugged. She didn't look amused, but Shane knew this was just how Regina was. Camilla would understand. He hoped.

Regina grabbed Alexi's hand and forced him to sit next to her on the couch. They were so close she was practically on his lap. As if memories of Marcus were now a distant past instead of days ago, she tossed one leg over his and played with his hair and watched Johann enter the basement.

"Good to see you, Johann," said Shane, greeting the oldest vampire in the room. Johann looked tired, which gave him an air of age even though his face still looked young. His long hair was pulled back in a low ponytail and his gangly frame moved slower than Shane had expected. Perhaps recent events just weighed heavily on his mind.

"Likewise." Johann smiled a cold smile and sat.

Shane gestured for everyone to join Regina, Alexi and Johann in finding a seat. All the leaders of former tribes were there, in some cases with their lieutenants.

"The Vampire Council is now called to order." Shane sat at the chair he had set at the front of the room. Everyone here considered him their leader, and this made him appear so, but he really wanted this to be a process where everyone's voice was heard.

"I'd like to talk about the betrayer," Luke said through narrow eyes.

Shane nodded to his best friend. He knew that was heavy on Luke's mind. He also knew that he had to do everything in his power to make sure that Luke was the one who got to kill Dimas when the time came. "Anyone else have a topic?"

Johann spoke up, his voice raspy and tired. "Hunting territories. I want to make sure it is clearly defined how we all split hunting grounds, now that we are one united tribe."

Shane nodded. "That's important."

Regina sat up straight, a little flirtatious smirk on her face. "I want to talk about the Dark Prophecy."

Shane was puzzled by this. Johann's and Luke's topics he'd expected, but not Regina's. "Oh?"

"Add it to the list, Shaney." She sat back and crossed her sexy legs. Camilla glared at her from across the room. She hated watching this gorgeous vampire flirting with her man, even if Shane did look completely unaffected by any of it.

"All right." Shane still looked confused, but he continued. "Is that all the topics for today?"

Camilla was nervous and felt like an outsider, but one item had been on her mind since the fateful night on the Oregon border. She raised her hand slowly, watching Shane carefully.

He smiled at her with kind eyes. He thought she looked adorable, and no one missed how he looked at her. "Of course, Camilla. What's your concern?"

"Theresa. I know her. She'll have spent every waking minute plotting her revenge and she could attack at any moment." Camilla swallowed hard. "We need to be prepared."

Isabelle stood up. "We? There is no we. We tolerate you but we don't trust you."

Shane put a hand up to Isabelle. He looked

around the room at the other vampires. They said nothing but he could see it in their eyes. They all felt the same as Isabelle. Even Luke didn't look completely ready to stand on Camilla's side. "Isabelle. Take a deep breath. I've always admired your passion, but Camilla is not the enemy here. Theresa is. And Camilla brings up a valid point. We'll add it to the list."

Isabelle sat back down, having the good graces to look a little embarrassed by her own outburst.

"So, if those are the topics, let's start with Dimas. We'll need intel on where he is," Shane said to start the council.

"I'll go hunting for him," Luke volunteered.

Shane shook his head, shutting him down. "Just intel at this point. No emotions."

Luke tried to hide how offended he was. "You don't trust me?"

Shane looked straight at his friend. "I don't trust Dimas. We'll find out where he is and what he's up to and then make a plan to bring him down. You will be the one to kill him. I swear to you on that."

Luke nodded, accepting that it might be all he could ask for. His whole life, human and vampire combined, Luke had always been more of a lover than a fighter. But he hated Dimas with every fiber of his being. He had hated him wholeheartedly before he stole Julianna's life and murdered her in front of his very eyes. Now? He wasn't sure there was a word strong enough to describe his overwhelming hatred.

"I can send scouts," Damian voiced. He was sitting next to Isabelle, one foot resting on the other knee. Shane noticed how relaxed he looked, which was a stark contrast to how high-strung he remembered him being. Perhaps this mission would be good for him.

"Thank you. Report back by the end of the week. We'll need to act fast to end his betraying." Shane's eyes narrowed at the thought of the skinny liar.

"Can we talk about the prophecy now?" Regina asked. She played with her hair as if she were bored with the topic of Dimas, even though he had played a part even in Marcus' death.

"What about the prophecy?" Shane looked from

Regina over to Luke, who raised an eyebrow in response. Camilla watched them all closely.

"I don't think it's been completely fulfilled," Regina stated flatly.

"How so?" Shane was truly curious. Was his part in all of this in question? Or was it simply not over? He realized in an instant that he really didn't know that much about the supposed prophecy. Perhaps he'd been too quick to put himself on the vampire throne.

Regina leaned forward and rested her elbows on her knees, her cleavage spilling out of her top. Camilla was certain Regina was squeezing a little extra just to make sure her breasts were on full display. "You were the one to save us, that much came true. But what about the second part?"

"You mean, the uniting of all vampire tribes?" Shane asked, slightly confused. Every once in a while, the fact that he was a new vampire was extremely obvious, and he shifted in his seat at how on display his newbornness felt at this moment.

Regina shook her head, a slight pout to her lips.

"I'm talking about the part where vampires are eradicated from the earth."

"What?" The word escaped Shane's lips before he could stop it. He'd never heard about an end to their species.

"I think the witches are going to do it." Regina looked right at Camilla and stared her down.

Camilla stood, breathing heavily, suddenly feeling very human in a room full of vampires. They all watched her without movement, but they felt like predators lying in wait.

Sensing her distress, Shane stood too. "Hold on now." He looked over at Luke, who leaned back and folded his arms. "Should we tell them?"

Luke smirked with playfulness that only Luke could muster at a time like this. "I suppose it couldn't hurt."

Shane sighed and looked at his feet. In a sense he was scared to tell them the truth about the prophecy. Everything they believed about him was a complete lie and he would have to admit that. But on the other hand, he knew this weight was too much for his shoulders and there would be a sense of relief at stepping down from a place he'd never had the right to hold. "The Dark Prophecy isn't real. Dimas made the whole thing up."

Regina looked at Shane with pity, like a mother who has to explain the way the world really works to a young teenager. "And who told you that? Dimas?"

Shane just stared at Luke as the realization came crashing down on them. Everything they knew about the prophecy they'd heard from Dimas. And everything they'd been taught to believe about it not being real came from Dimas. The Betrayer. A proven, compulsive liar.

Johann chuckled, but it wasn't in an offensive way. He was the elder here and he felt the need to set the history books straight. "I can assure you emphatically that Dimas did not invent the Dark Prophecy. It predates him by centuries."

Luke leaned forward and flashed his debonair, Hollywood smile. "Well, well. Isn't this enlightening? So Shane is the chosen one, after all. And I'll bet Dimas just couldn't handle that it wasn't *him*. As if. Oh, I can't wait to end that guy!"

"Boys." Regina clapped her hands to bring their attention back to her. Shane slowly sat back down and Regina continued. "Wherever the Dark Prophecy came from, I think we all know now that it's real. The first part already came true. So now how do we stop the second part of the prophecy? Vampires gone from this earth. Tragic."

Camilla tried to keep her face impassive, but she couldn't help but let a tiny thought into her mind that maybe it wasn't so tragic after all.

"Can we stop it?" Shane looked at Johann, relying on his wisdom for guidance.

Johann shrugged. "As the story goes, a powerful vampire would come along—you, of course—and unite the vampires bringing peace to the tribes and ending the Shadow Wars. Done. But then slowly, like a fog creeping in, one by one vampires would start to disappear until the species goes extinct. Does this happen in a month? A year? A century? I have no idea.

Can we stop it?" Johann looked around at all the faces watching him. Some young, some old, but none wanting to be eradicated from the earth. "I somehow doubt it."

"Bullshit!" This time Regina stood. She pointed at Camilla. "A fog rolling in? A plague overtaking us? It's witches! And *she* knows how we can stop it."

Camilla shook her head. "I know nothing about a curse that will eradicate vampires, I swear."

Shane stood to match Regina and again to protect Camilla. His chair flew out from behind him and went too fast and too far to just be inertia. Alexi watched the chair screech across the floor and bang against the back wall, a loud reminder of his unparalleled power. "She's one of us now, Regina."

"She's not. I don't see any fangs! What's the good of having a witch as a pet if you aren't going to even use her to protect your own kind!?"

"No one is using Camilla and she's not a vampire because I didn't want to turn her." Shane kept his voice controlled, but the anger was there simmering just below the surface. If the witches were trying to introduce a plague that would kill all vampires slowly, Camilla would never be safe in this compound.

Alexi pulled gently on Regina's arm, trying to diffuse the standoff. He'd survived for centuries for knowing his place—not a talent that Regina had ever cultivated. In one flick of his wrist, Shane could burn Regina to a crisp where she stood, and Alexi well knew it. Never anger a powerful vampire when it comes to the woman he loves.

Regina slowly sat back down, catching the hint, but still glaring at Camilla. Camilla stood next to Shane and grabbed his hand.

She cleared her throat. "Regina's right. My loyalty now is to Shane. And if there is something I can do to stop Theresa and her curses, I will not hesitate to do it. Whether I am a vampire or not."

Regina crossed her legs and rested her hand on Alexi's knee. "Now we're getting somewhere."

Isabelle leaned forward and spoke to Regina as if Camilla weren't even in the room. "You trust her?"

Regina smiled. "Whether I trust her or not, I do

think she's our only chance. We'll need a witch in our corner to fight witchcraft."

Johann shook his head. "The prophecy says nothing about witchcraft. The threat could come from anywhere."

Regina snorted. "Dimas was stupid enough to bring the witches into the Shadow Wars. And now we've made a powerful enemy. The prophecy plays right into everything that's happened."

"I believe you," Shane stated. Regina looked up, pleased that she was making headway. "Theresa certainly hates us enough and certainly has the power to create a plague that would slowly kill us all. It does sound a lot like witchcraft." He looked over at Camilla. "Camilla and I will work together to find a way to stop the second part of the Prophecy."

Regina spread her arms and said, "That's all I ask."

Johann sensed that topic had run its course, so he announced, "Now. About hunting territories. I think they should be clearly outlined on a map, so we don't get right back to where we were during the Shadow Wars."

"Wait a minute, Johann." Damian leaned forward. "If we're one tribe now, doesn't that mean that we're all free to hunt wherever we want to?"

"That will be complete anarchy!" Johann countered.

Shane pinched the tip of his nose. He'd always hated politics.

"I've already drawn up boundaries," Shane announced. He then looked at Damian. "This is to protect the humans and vampires. Keep the balance. I want everything spread out so we remain undetected and one area doesn't get ravished by our hunger."

"I'll hand out the maps when you leave," Elias announced. There were nods around the room. Damian looked a little upset but not enough to voice any more concerns.

And then there was a flash of light and a puff of smoke. Camilla jumped as Theresa appeared in the center of the room, vampires seated all around her.

At the sight of the evil witch, Regina hissed and

fangs and claws extended all around the room. Elias and Isabelle both took a fighting stance. Shane still held Camilla's hand and stared, almost no reaction at all. Of course, everyone knew he didn't need claws to fight.

"Relax. I'm not really here. This is just a projection," Theresa announced. "But I am excited that I timed everything so well. All my favorites in one place. Even you, Camilla."

Camilla swallowed hard and inched closer to Shane, but she said nothing in response.

"What do you want, Theresa?" Shane asked, his voice calm but firm.

"I want my daughter back," Theresa said flatly.

"Don't you mean your stepdaughter? You didn't seem that interested in the mountains," Luke responded.

Theresa narrowed her eyes at Luke but then ignored him, as if he were just an annoying cockroach and not worth her time to step on. "I want to make a trade."

"What kind of trade?" Shane asked.

Isabelle shook her head at Shane, warning him off. And Camilla straight out said no, but Shane continued to look at Theresa.

"You give me Kara and I'll give you Julianna," Theresa smiled.

Luke jumped up. "Julianna is dead."

"Kara is more dead than Julianna," Theresa lifted her head defiantly, as if she were offended.

Shane began to clear his mind and he could sense there was a twisted truth to her words. He could also sense something was afoot, but he wanted to focus on Julianna. What had the witch done with his sister? "Explain yourself, witch."

The projection of Theresa turned right and waved someone over. Shane saw blonde curls before he saw her fully and gasped at the sight. And then his sister, or some evil twin of his sister because he couldn't figure out how it was done, stood in front of him.

"Julianna," Luke whispered.

The room was still. Julianna stood before them, maybe not in flesh and blood, and they knew their eyes couldn't be trusted against a witch's deception, but there she stood very much alive.

"Please, Shane." Camilla tried to protect him. She didn't know what Theresa was up to completely, but she knew it was a trap of some sort.

Shane wanted to seek the truth, but he couldn't stop his emotions from controlling him. There before him stood his sister—and he had seen her head severed from her body by Dimas in this very room a week ago. He was stunned into silence like everyone else. He swallowed the lump that was forming in his chest, wanting this to be real—and at the same time being terrified that it wasn't.

Julianna looked at Luke with sad eyes. "Why? Why did you murder me?"

"What?" Luke was overcome by confusion. Was she really standing before him? Was she really accusing him of her murder?

Theresa shoved Julianna out of the projection, as if she were afraid of what else she might say.

Shane's eyes narrowed as Luke remained frozen

in shock. "Are you harboring Dimas?" Shane demanded, suddenly deciding that he must be the puppeteer at the heart of all this.

"Do we have an agreement?" Theresa demanded, ignoring his question about Dimas.

And somehow at this, Shane was able to burst out of the shackles of shock and deception that Theresa had thrown around the room with her entrance. He knew her ruse with clarity.

"My God, Luke, this is a diversion!" Shane pushed his arms toward Theresa's projection and an unseen force shoved the image and it dissipated. And then, with no further explanation, he ran out of the room and up the stairs at vampire speed.

Luke looked around the room at many shocked vampire faces, some with their fangs still hanging out.

Only Isabelle had her wits about her. "Go, you idiot!" She gestured toward the door Shane had just run out of.

Luke hesitated a moment, still processing everything. A diversion? Julianna? Murderer? But then he realized he trusted Shane and wasn't sure what else he could trust, so he ran after him with Isabelle at his side.

They didn't move as fast as they could, but the other vampires at the council soon followed as well. They didn't want to be left alone with witches, for one. And they wanted to know what the hell was going on, for another.

All the way to the fourth floor, Luke and Isabelle ran behind Shane. And they heard the scuffle before they saw it. Shane was fighting someone in Kara's room. Isabelle sprang immediately into action, her long black ponytail flying behind her. She was always one to act before thinking.

Luke slowed a bit in the doorway with heaviness weighing down his limbs, Shane's words sinking in. The vision of Julianna was a diversion.

The witches were kidnapping Kara.

7

Julianna was shaken by everything happening all around her. Something told her not to trust the women who had saved her. Perhaps it was the way Theresa was still standing there laughing at the vampires. Or perhaps it was the looks on Luke's and Shane's faces when they saw her. She didn't see the look of someone who had murdered her. Had it all been a lie?

The sudden disappearance of half a dozen witches did nothing to calm her nerves.

A shaft of moonlight peeked through the windows near the roof of the warehouse. Now that the sun had set, Dimas didn't have to stay hidden in the shadows. He sat on a pile of boxes as if it were a throne, and he watched Julianna pace around the warehouse floor. He did look regal, sitting up tall, his chin held high.

Julianna caught his eye and a memory popped back into her brain. She remembered being a newborn vampire and not having any clue how to control her overwhelming thirst. She remembered wanting to ravage cities and rip throats out. She clutched her own throat, slightly repulsed at the memory. But then she remembered Dimas. He had been there for her then and so many other countless times. He was a mentor and a friend.

The worry softened from her face as she watched the white-haired vampire sitting upon the boxes. He said nothing but tensed as if he were afraid of her.

"What are you thinking, Lord Dimas?" Julianna smiled and walked over to where he sat.

He tentatively grabbed her hands and held them in his upon his lap. "No one calls me Lord anymore. It's nice to hear. Especially on your lips."

Julianna didn't pull away. He was familiar, comfortable. She felt secure in his presence, something she didn't feel around Theresa with no clue as to why.

"Why does no one call you Lord anymore? Aren't you still leading our tribe?"

The way she said "our tribe" made Dimas feel warm inside and sad at the same time. He didn't want to tell her that their tribe was no more, but he did want to continue spitting the poison that Theresa had started spreading. Dimas sighed. "Sadly, no. After he murdered you, Luke and Shane tried to kill me but I escaped."

There. The second part wasn't even a lie.

Julianna looked up at the ceiling, as if it might carry answers to things she could no longer see clearly for herself. "That doesn't sound like Luke and my brother. Why would they want to kill us?" Something clicked in her brain. Every once in a while a thought or memory would just pop back in. "The prophecy? Were they fighting the prophecy? Did it come true?"

Dimas shifted uncomfortably in his seat. Julianna had always believed in Shane as the vampire from the Dark Prophecy. There was no way he wanted her to know how right she'd been about her brother. "It has not come true yet. And yes, your brother has done nothing but fight everything you stood for. Everything you did for him. He's done nothing but resist."

Julianna let one hand fall to her side. Sadness overtook confusion. "But, why?"

"Perhaps..." Dimas licked his lips and carefully thought about what he was trying to say. "Perhaps you were wrong about him? Perhaps there is another?"

Julianna shook her head, her blonde curls bouncing all around her. "No. It's Shane. I've always known it." She pulled on Dimas' hand. "Come on. We need to go talk to Shane and Luke. Not through witchcraft and projections, but face to face."

Dimas' eyes opened wide with alarm. He couldn't have her go to them. They might bring back memories he didn't want her to have. "No!" he said a little too quickly. And then tried to recover with, "It's far too dangerous."

"It is?" Julianna asked, again feeling like her brain was murky where details were concerned. Would they try to kill her again?

"Julianna, I've always cared about you." Dimas took a bold move and placed a hand on Julianna's cheek. Again, she didn't pull away. "You have to be careful who you trust. They killed you easily when you were a vampire. In your human state, you'll be easy prey."

Julianna leaned into Dimas' hand upon her cheek. She stood up against his legs, one hand still resting in his. He was right that she was vulnerable as a human, but she still couldn't muster the fear of her brother. And something told her heart that Luke cared for her. But Dimas had always supported her. He had always taken care of her. He was the one she'd always trusted. If he warned her they were dangerous, she would listen.

"So, what do we do now?" Julianna asked in a soft voice.

"Stay with me," Dimas said, looking straight into her eyes. "I can take care of you."

And she knew it was true. He'd been her Lord and protector throughout her vampire life. When he leaned in to kiss her, she wasn't surprised, but something just didn't feel right. His cold lips pressed against hers and she didn't pull away. She cared about Dimas, didn't she? As she stood there debating how she felt about the kiss, he moved his lips to her jawline. She let him. He kissed down to her neck, and he heard the pulse beating in her artery. His fangs extended and he whispered, "And I can make you a vampire again."

At this, Julianna pulled away. She was shocked even to hear her own voice say it out loud. "I don't want to be a vampire again."

The lust faded from Dimas' eyes and was quickly replaced by anger. Even trapped and brainwashed, he couldn't control her. He jumped off the pile of boxes, fangs still extended. Through her human eyes, Dimas looked like the creature of the night you hear tell about. He stalked slowly toward her, rage in his eyes, venom dripping from his sharp fangs.

She continued slowly backing away.

"There's no life for you as a human, Julianna," he said slowly, his voice almost a growl. "With me, you can start over. Away from all this." He gestured toward the warehouse and the small gathering of witches.

"Please, Lord Dimas. I do want to start over. But not as a vampire." Her hands were up protectively, even though she knew if he lunged, she'd have no way to stop him. How could she reason with him? He'd always been reasonable, hadn't he? This was Dimas, her Lord and protector. "I'll go with you. I will. Just let me be human."

Dimas thought about everything he had done, backstabbed and sabotaged to get where he was now. He had even stooped so low as to consort with witches! And he only ever wanted two things: to be the vampire from the Prophecy and to have Julianna at his side as he ruled them all. It might be too late for the prophecy—too many vampires already pledged their loyalty to Shane—but Julianna could still be his. But he snarled as he watched her sniveling pleas. He didn't want a frail human. He wanted the fierce vampire she'd always been.

He saw the horror on her face the moment he lunged. She knew what was coming. She screamed as he grabbed her and pierced her neck with his fangs. But after two pulls, she became limp in his arms and the futile resistance was gone. Dimas tried to stay focused on the task at hand, but he did smile to himself even as he drained her life force. He should be able to brainwash her again once she turned, and they would live forevermore side by side. Maybe he couldn't have *everything* he wanted, but he could have Julianna, the beautiful blonde vampire who had always looked up to him. What a prize. And turning her against her own brother? Just the icing on the delectable cake.

But his thoughts were cut short as a gust of power blew him off Julianna and back against the boxes where he'd been sitting a moment ago. The boxes flew in every direction even as Julianna fell lifelessly to the ground. Dimas looked up from the ground to see Theresa bounding toward him, her arm in the air post-incantation, and a murderous look on her face.

"How dare you!" Theresa shouted at Dimas as he scrambled to his feet, wiping Julianna's blood from his lips. To the coven members who remained in the warehouse, she instructed, "Help her."

Dimas extended claws and fangs, preparing for a fight. "I took your potion. You can't kill me."

From three feet away, Theresa raised her hand in the air and Dimas shot up, feet dangling as if she were holding him although she hadn't laid a physical finger on him. "These are my spells, you jackass. Anything that is done can be undone. And I think you've served your purpose. You're more a threat now than an asset." She pinched her fingers together and Dimas felt his throat tightening and collapsing. He didn't need air, but he was certain she could snap his neck right off.

"Theresa!" one of the ladies shouted. "The vampires figured it out and are fighting back."

"I trust Elyse and I'm taking out the garbage right now." Theresa squeezed even harder on Dimas' neck.

"Elyse is down. She might be hurt," the witch who was still watching the projection explained.

Theresa's head snapped back. "What?" She loosened her grip on Dimas through the distraction and he fell back to the ground, clutching his throat as he fell.

Damned vampires!

Through the projection she watched the fighting in Kara's room take place inside the vampire compound. She looked at Julianna, limp and lifeless on the floor of the warehouse. And she saw Camilla, still in the basement where the council had been. "Shit." She couldn't save all three at once.

Turning back to Dimas, she spoke low and controlled, though her tone dripped with fury and her intent was made very clear. "Our deal is off. If I see you near Julianna or any of my witches again, I. Will. Kill. You."

And she vanished into the thin air, her threat still hanging over Dimas like a dark cloud.

He stood slowly, still rubbing his throat. He watched the remaining Harbor Coven witches as they raised Julianna's body and laid her on the table she'd been revitalized on earlier in the day. All he had to do was force Julianna to drink his blood and then they'd be powerless to stop his plan. She'd be a vampire again within days.

The witches worked feverishly to save Julianna's life with the rejuvenating potion and incantation they'd all used to survive battles with the vampires. She was the newest member of the coven, even if she hadn't done the induction ceremony yet. She was one of them and they would save her, treating her as one of their own. No one was paying attention to Dimas. In fact, most of the witches didn't think of him one way or another. He was just a means to an end. An item to be used and discarded.

They continued working. And he crept closer. Silently. And in the shadows. One step at a time. No sudden movements.

Julianna lay there like a sleeping princess from a fairytale. Her blonde hair fanned out all around beneath her. Her perfect nose pointed up to the sky. Her skin was alabaster, barely any sign of life to her tone. If he could just get to her and force his blood upon her, he could steal her away. He'd awaken his princess in a few days and they would ride off, vampire and prize.

But there were half a dozen witches. And even

though they were all busy grabbing ingredients, mixing potion, preparing Julianna's body, at any given time someone was facing Julianna. Or facing her enough that they would see him coming. He'd never get enough blood down her throat before they stopped him.

Dimas looked all around the warehouse. Thank goodness Theresa and Elyse had left. They were the only two witches who he actually thought, one on one, could stop him. But six against one? He still needed a distraction.

With vampire speed, so fast he was but a blur across the room, Dimas sped to the red door at the front of the warehouse. It had to be big. Big enough to get all six witches away from Julianna. He looked left and then right and then he saw it. There was a forklift already aimed at shelving that housed many of the witches' ghastly ingredients. He shoved the forklift with all his vampiric strength. He'd never been a warrior and he was far too skinny to be considered strong, but even he with his skinny arms was superhuman in strength.

And it worked. The forklift shot toward the

shelving and crashed loudly when it connected. Items shattered and the shelf itself teetered back and then forward before falling on the forklift.

Every witch looked over. Dimas sped quickly back into the shadows as he watched the witches run over to the shelf. All but one, he noticed. A pretty witch with long black hair remained at Julianna's side. But it would have to do. He would have no better chance.

He bolted past the pretty witch, blowing her hair back as he ran past, fast as lightning toward Julianna. The witch turned and tried to react, but her reaction time was far slower than a vampire's.

He'd have to carry out the rest of his plan later, forcing Julianna to drink his blood in another locale. Time was precious, but he was outnumbered here. He had to run. Dimas lifted Julianna off the table and ran out the back door as fast as he could. And none of the witches could stop him.

8

"Careful! She's got Kara!" Shane shouted at Isabelle as she flew into the bedroom on the third floor with fangs and claws extended.

Isabelle was a warrior, through and through, and one of the fiercest fighters Shane had ever seen, human or vampire. Her long black hair and boots and look of pure destruction were a sharp contrast to the soft, cream-colored bedroom she was attacking in.

Shane recognized Emily as Kara's human sister seconds before Isabelle kicked her in the chest, sending her flying toward the wall.

This action sent Elyse, Theresa's second-in-command, straight into action. "Teleport out of here! I've got Kara!" And Shane knew he didn't have much time before they left with Kara. And he had no idea what they planned to do with her, but he doubted it was with good intentions.

Elyse gripped Kara's arms, holding her hostage in front of her. Thoughts of burning Elyse again like he'd done in the forest crept into Shane's mind, but he couldn't risk hurting Kara. But then again, he needed to stop underestimating his newest vampire. The witches had been able to capture her because they'd taken her by surprise, but whatever was happening, Kara wasn't going willingly.

Out of the corner of his eye, Shane saw Luke trying to get to Kara, but a witch stood in his way and he swiped claws at her arm. She threw him backward with a flick of her wrist. He got up and kept coming, but Shane knew time was ticking.

Emily had already vanished from the room, leaving Isabelle to turn her skills on another witch, who tossed Isabelle backward before disappearing herself.

Shane focused on Elyse. The second Kara pulled away from her captor with a little shove, Shane sent a fireburst at Elyse that quickly engulfed her. The look of shock transitioned to a look of horror, and then she flailed her arms even as she lit the room aglow, covered as she was head to toe with fire. Luke, Shane and Isabelle watched the witch burn, knowing she could not be killed this way, just severely injured. But Kara jumped into action. Ignoring the flames, she jumped on Elyse's burning back and twisted her head, severing it completely, with just her two hands, from her neck. Kara hopped down and tossed the flaming head to the floor, and Shane quickly summoned water to put the two fires, one on the body and one on the head, out. What remained when this was over were two piles of ashes.

Elyse was finally dead. At Kara's hands.

Luke ran to Kara and embraced her. She welcomed the comfort.

Johann and Damian appeared in the doorway just in time to see the aftermath.

"What happened?" Johann asked, wide-eyed, looking from the ash to the young vampire, to Shane and

Isabelle. Damian also stared, arms folded across his chest, unable to make heads or tails of what occurred.

"Kara just beheaded a witch we all thought was unkillable," Shane explained.

Kara pulled away from Luke and demanded the attention from the room. "They were kidnapping me to take me back to their coven." Kara looked right at Shane. "My sister, Emily, is a witch now."

Shane quickly understood how Kara could have been so overwhelmed and overpowered. One moment she'd been hanging out in her room, the next she was being kidnapped by an enemy that now included her sister.

Shane cleared his mind to see the truth, trusting in his power to fill in the gaps. A moment later he announced, "They were trying to kill you." Kara didn't look as shocked as Shane expected. He locked eyes with Luke. "This has something to do with Julianna."

"Dimas is there. I know he is. Who else would tell Julianna that *I* murdered her?" Luke was calm, but the anger on his face was apparent.

Shane nodded. "He is. He brought Julianna to the witches."

Luke, still holding Kara like a father comforting a child, responded. "We'll need to go in and save her." He turned his chin down to face Kara. In such a short time, he and Shane had come to think of her as family. Like a little sister. "We'll get your sister too."

Kara pulled back and a ferocity took over her. Her face and mannerisms looked far older than her fourteen years, even as her body still looked so young. "No. Emily is a witch now. There's nothing to save."

"You could turn her." Damian's voice filled the cream-colored bedroom. All eyes turned toward him. "Witches are still human. She could become a vampire and then she would no longer be your mortal enemy."

Kara looked up at Shane for his support. He folded his arms across his chest, matching Damian. He thought about it. It was definitely an option, but would it be hypocritical after refusing to let Camilla turn? He hated seeing sisters forced into becoming mortal enemies, though. Shane studied Kara's face, still round from youth. "Is that what you would want?"

Kara looked around the room at her new family. She had muddied memories of a loving human father who had tried his best to raise two girls after the loss of his wife. But that seemed so long ago, despite it being just a week. This was her life now. This was her family. And she loved being a vampire. She had taken to it so naturally. Shane was like her new father and Luke her older brother. Isabelle was someone she wanted to be like one day, standing there ready to fight even when the enemy was vanquished. The two vampires in the doorway were new to her, but even they looked ready to lay down their lives for her.

Shane knew the answer before Kara said it. He didn't even need his powers, as it was written across her face.

"Okay. Let's go get Julianna and Emily. But we'll have to kill Theresa," Kara announced, a look of darkness passing across her eyes.

Isabelle nodded, her long black hair swaying with the movement. "Already part of the plan."

"So I guess the Council topic of what to do about Theresa has now been discussed," Luke smirked, one eyebrow raised.

"Camilla was right. She's been plotting this whole time," Shane smiled back at Luke. "But even though she struck first, we'll strike harder. And end this once and for all." He turned back to the vampires in the doorway. "I promised vampires peace, and this is the only way we'll get it."

All the vampires nodded in agreement.

Johann, with his scratchy voice and calm demeanor, asked, "Will we be killing *all* the witches? Or just Theresa and turn the rest?"

Shane opened his mouth to answer, but it was Kara who spoke. "Kill them."

Shane looked from Kara to Isabelle. They were too much alike.

Isabelle shrugged. "I really like this girl."

"This time Isabelle may be right." Luke flashed his debonair smile, "They'll most likely remain loyal to Theresa and even as vampires we won't be able to trust them."

"Okay, I thought it, but I didn't say it this time." Isabelle stared back at Luke. "Kara said to kill them."

"Well, you're all right," Shane answered. Twice now either Theresa or her witches had invaded their compound. They couldn't just live in peace with a volatile enemy, always plotting. "They can't be trusted. Once Kara and Emily are safely out of there, I'll burn their coven."

"After I kill Dimas," Luke jumped in.

"And I kill Theresa," Isabelle added.

"*I'm* killing Theresa," Kara quickly responded.

"You can both kill Theresa." Shane stuck a hand up to keep the peace between the bloodthirsty women.

"How do we find them?" Johann asked.

"Her coven meets at her hair salon," Shane announced. The words were out of his mouth before he thought about it, but the truth was there.

Kara nodded. "That makes sense. She spends quite a bit of time there for someone who's never made an honest day's wages in her life."

"I'll gather vampires from my compound." Damian carefully avoided using the word tribe, even though it was still how he really thought about the vampires he lived with. In the short time since the vampires had been united, not enough had changed for him to stop thinking of the old ways.

"No, I'd rather do this quietly." Shane looked at Damian and then added, "But thank you."

Damian nodded in response.

"Isabelle, Kara, Luke and I will enter. Isabelle and Kara are responsible for Theresa. Luke, you take care of Dimas and I'll help you, if need be, but my primary mission is getting Julianna. Damian, you and Johann are welcome to come but I understand if you don't want to." Shane looked at them for their answer.

"Theresa and her witches attacked me unprovoked." Johann lifted a weary chin. "And I still owe her for Bronwyn's death."

"And I don't like the fact we will never know peace if the betrayer remains alive," Damian added.

"What about Regina and Alexi? Did they leave?"

Shane looked over their shoulder and, as if on cue, Regina came running up behind Johann and Damian in the doorway. She was holding Alexi's hand and stared straight at Shane. He knew instantly that something was wrong and ran to the doorway.

"Alexi and I were..." She looked coyly at Alexi, as if it somehow made it less obvious what they'd been doing. It did not. "We stopped to take a break and we heard everything." She looked from Alexi to Shane and her face changed dramatically. She now had the look of a bearer of bad news. "Camilla's gone, Shane. And she went willingly with Theresa."

Shane half-whispered, "What?" before he ran out the bedroom door and flew down the stairs, all the way to the basement meeting room. Luke and Isabelle followed, but no one else did. The others felt it was a violation of his privacy, having been so betrayed by someone he cared about. Luke wanted to be there for Shane and Isabelle wanted to make sure there was not still an imminent threat.

But there was none.

Even as Shane knew the truth before he saw it with his own eyes.

Camilla was gone. And she'd left willingly with Theresa.

9

"You served me well, Camilla," Theresa said with a smile. She paced her bedroom overlooking the ocean. The lights were out, but a soft glow of moonlight created a haze around the room. Camilla could make out the waves crashing in the distance and saw a neatly made bed in a clean and well-kept bedroom. Photos of a smiling happy family lined the shelves and end tables.

"My pleasure, Theresa," Camilla smiled. "But I was really earning their trust. You should have let me stay."

"Your work there is done. When Shane and his little band of monsters come to save you and Julianna, as they will inevitably do, then I will kill them. I kind of want to stake them in their hearts just so they can watch everything as they die, but it would be faster and easier to just use magic," Theresa debated aloud.

Camilla nodded wordlessly.

Near the large sliding glass door, the moonlight was brightest, but in the far reaches of the room, there were multitudes of shadows. In these pockets of shadows, Camilla imagined all sorts of evil could be lurking. The shadows were where Theresa did her best work. Ironic that she was so obsessed with destroying creatures of the night.

Camilla turned to Theresa. "Where is Rich?"

She noticed Theresa wasn't her usual put-together self. She looked as if she hadn't slept in days and her dark hair, normally tightly pulled back into a twist or a bun, was half-up and half resting on her shoulders.

Theresa snorted. "He's down on skid row looking for Kara, the dumbass." Again, she was uncharacteristically agitated, as if it were all falling apart. "I should have killed him when I had the chance. This is what happens when you get soft."

Camilla smiled at her leader's perceived weakness. "You actually love him."

Theresa paced over to the window, choosing to watch the violence of the ocean waves rather than the judgment of Camilla. "Don't be ridiculous. I just didn't want to break Emily's heart."

Camilla joined Theresa at the window. "Since when do you care about a young girl's heart?"

Theresa turned to Camilla and stared at her sharply. "And since when do you dare to judge me?"

Camilla watched Theresa, falling apart before her eyes, and wondered at her own emboldening. Had she learned to speak openly subconsciously from the vampires? "Why are we here, Theresa? Why did you bring me to your home?"

Theresa waved a hand at Camilla as if to say the question was meaningless, but the flash in her eyes belied her dismissiveness. Camilla could see the truth. Theresa was losing control.

"We'll need to get back to the salon soon, but I wanted to talk to you alone first," Theresa finally responded. Her eyes became distant and Camilla decided it was best not to speak. She waited for Theresa to voice her thoughts. "I was twenty. When I became a witch. I was twenty." Camilla startled at the change of subject. Theresa had never spoken of the old days before. What was prompting this? "He was handsome. And kind. And I loved to just be around him." She sighed. "I fell head over heels. But my family was a bunch of poor farmers. Sheep farmers to be exact. And he was from a prominent family. One of the ones that ran our small town in the New World. There was no way he would have looked at me without witchcraft. I've always been beautiful, but those were the days when you had to be in the right class too. And then my mother got sick."

Theresa turned to Camilla, her face sad at the memory. Camilla just listened. She'd always been good at knowing when to hold her tongue. Theresa continued. "If my mother died, my father surely would've married me off as fast as possible. Women didn't live independently back then, and he saw me as either a servant or a pawn. And so I knew I had very little time to win the heart of the nobleman I loved. As I was, he might have slept with me, but he would never have married me. So when the old hag offered me the potions, I took no time in deciding to sell my soul. I danced for the devil in the moonlight, bathing in blood. And I found that I liked it. I liked it very much. A woman's lot in the 1600's was to marry, cook, clean, pop out babies. Basically, just servants and nursemaids. But with magic I had power. And I loved having power."

"What about your mother? Hadn't you tried to save your mother?" Camilla remembered the story Theresa had always told.

"Partially true." Theresa huffed a laugh at the noble lie she'd created. "My mom *did* get sick and I *did* try to save her with magic. But I became a witch to marry the man I loved. That was the real reason. And then guess what? He slept with Annabelle. The minute he suspected I was a witch, he fell instantly out of love with me. He was the first person I ever killed with my own two hands." She shook her head at the sad turn of events in her memory. "And that was when I learned about betrayal. And what a dangerous emotion love was. It had made me the fool."

Camilla didn't know what to say. "I guess that's good you learned the lesson so young?"

Theresa smiled at Camilla in response. "Did you give Shane the hex bag?"

"I did."

Theresa let a small smile creep across her lips. "And did he take it willingly?"

Camilla nodded, remembering Shane's handsome face as he'd delighted in her gift. "He did."

Then Theresa made a sound Camilla never thought she'd hear from a centuries-old witch. Theresa giggled. "We just may be able to end these goddamned monsters, after all." Theresa rubbed Camilla's arm in a loving, motherly way. "Thank you for your sacrifice. If you hadn't been so quick on your feet... Well, I don't know what I would have done without your spying." She pulled Camilla in for a hug, smoothing down her soft, brown hair. "You're such a great little witch."

The sound of footsteps pulled them away from their embrace and turned their attention to the doorway of Theresa's bedroom. Emily stood there with a dark-skinned witch called Henna. They looked frazzled and upset.

"There you are!" Emily bounded into the room and turned on the light, momentarily blinding Theresa and Camilla. "We've been looking everywhere for you."

Theresa was suddenly very suspicious. "Can I not leave a coven of witches for a few minutes with a vampire and not be able to trust you?"

Emily and Henna shared a glance, and then Henna swallowed. Hard. "It's not just the betrayer," Henna explained.

Theresa stepped forward, her face the mask of hardness and cold calculation she normally wore. The true Theresa, the one with anguish and frustration that had let her guard down in front of Camilla, was gone in an instant. "Did Julianna die?"

Henna shook her head. "I don't think so."

Theresa looked from Henna to Emily with a

stare so piercing it could stop your heart. "Then what *happened*?"

Henna took a moment too long to answer and Emily could see Theresa's face contorting with anger, so she stepped in to cut to the chase. "We didn't come to find you because of Julianna. She's gone. We came to find you because of Kara and Elyse." Emily took a moment to steel her resolve, rubbing the spot where Isabelle had kicked her a few minutes ago. "Kara stayed with the vampires and"—she looked at the floor— "Elyse is dead."

Whatever Henna and Emily had expected from Theresa, it wasn't the laughter that escaped her throat. She looked maniacal, hair slightly disheveled and laughing at her misfortune. After a moment, she responded, "That's impossible. Elyse can't die."

Emily nodded. "Elyse is dead. They beheaded her while she was burning."

Camilla stepped forward. "Shane is very powerful."

Theresa's next response was more in line with

their expectations. She screamed. And then started picking up any object she could find and throwing it against the wall. Picture frames. A hair brush. A lamp. Some shoes that hadn't made it to the closet. Anything within reach was a victim.

After a few minutes of tirade, Theresa ran her fingers through her dark hair, as if calming herself down, but it actually made her hair look more out of control than before. She had the wild look of someone on the razor's edge of insanity. "Then we kill Julianna. We just kill her. You take one of mine, I take one of yours." Theresa began pacing. "And we'll make him watch. Somehow, we'll get Shane, that little fucker, and we'll make him watch as I slowly, painfully, rip his sister into pieces!"

"Theresa." Emily practically shouted her stepmother's name, trying to break through. "Julianna and the betrayer are gone. Somehow, we'd have to find them in order to kill her. Wouldn't it be easier to attack the vampires again?"

Theresa's eyes became murderous. She stuck

her arm straight out in front of her and lifted Emily high against the wall without touching her, Emily's feet kicking the air uselessly beneath her—a repeat of the maneuver she had used on Dimas earlier in the day. "Easy? You've been a witch for one day! You know nothing of how I've plotted and planned. And they keep taking everything away from me!"

Emily gurgled from the choking force pressing up against her throat. Theresa was going to kill her. Henna stared on, too afraid to speak lest she be next, but Camilla was brave enough to rest a calming hand on Theresa's shoulder.

"Theresa," Camilla spoke softly in her tender voice. "Emily is not the enemy. Let's focus our anger."

Theresa turned to Camilla and looked at her with empty eyes, Emily still dangling from Theresa's angry power.

Camilla tugged gently again on Theresa's arm. She knew this was a tense situation and she approached it like someone would approach a tiger on the hunt. Calmly. Soothingly. Placating. "Let's regroup and figure out what we want to do to the *vampires*." Slowly she lowered Theresa's arm, and as she did, Emily slid down slowly to the floor, coughing and rubbing her throat when her feet finally reached solid ground.

Theresa was not remorseful. "Let that be a lesson to you, young witch." She spoke sternly at Emily, hunched over and trying to catch her breath beneath Theresa. "This is my coven and I call the shots. If I want to kill someone slowly you will nod and say 'yes, ma'am.'"

Emily rubbed her throat and stared at her stepmother but said nothing.

The tension in the room was stifling. Even the distant sound of ocean waves crashing couldn't relax the shoulders of the four witches gathered in the beach house bedroom.

Nervously, Henna spoke. "If you want me to find Julianna and the betrayer, I'll go." Henna was one hundred and twenty-two years old and always wore her hair pulled back into tiny braids with beads in it. She was classy, almost as classy as Theresa, and dressed impeccably. Walking by her on the streets, people would think professional woman. She was the furthest thing from the witches you see in Hollywood movies. But still, her confidence must have been a façade because she cowered now before her coven leader.

"Yes. Go." Theresa kicked Emily's foot for good measure. "And take this little brat with you. And I don't want to see either of your faces again unless you have Julianna with you."

Henna grabbed Emily's hand as an older sister would and led her from the room. Emily didn't care so much about Julianna and wasn't thrilled about going, but having felt her stepmother's power firsthand, she wasn't too keen on staying either. She wanted to remain focused on saving her sister, but Theresa's petty revenge kept getting them into trouble. Who cared about Dimas and Julianna?

And she was getting sick of it.

Emily left the room with Henna, but her mind was racing with her own agenda and how to keep it moving forward. She was going to need to learn to be a better witch. And fast.

As the two witches left to go find Shane's sister, Theresa stared at the mess all around her room from her tirade. She sighed, still remorseless, but with a swipe of her finger everything was put back together and set back in its place. If Richard did ever decide to come home, he would never suspect a thing.

Her heart squeezed a bit. Perhaps she did miss him. Perhaps a small part of her did care for him. She suddenly longed for a potion that could turn back time to when she was a wife and mother and Richard doted on Theresa's every move.

Camilla didn't want to be the first to speak, since Theresa's emotions were still so high. She watched her set her room back to the way it had been when they first transported here from Shane's compound, letting Theresa drive the conversation from here.

When Theresa didn't speak or move to leave, but instead sat upon the bed in thought, Camilla was surprised. She thought for sure Theresa would be eager to get back to the salon. Camilla sat on the bed next to

Theresa and smoothed out the soft gray comforter beneath her. Looking around the room, Camilla felt a little sorry for Theresa, although she would never say it out loud. This was the room of a happy family woman, a mother and wife. And yet, here sat a washed-up witch whose plans had all fallen apart and who couldn't see straight past her anger and vengeance.

She had already lost a daughter. Probably lost her husband. Almost killed her other daughter tonight. Lost her best friend, Elyse. Not sure where her collateral, Julianna, was. For the most powerful witch in Southern California, Theresa sure seemed a sad story.

"Remember when I first found you?" Theresa stared at Camilla. Camilla nodded, still letting Theresa drive the conversation. Theresa shook her head. "You were mousier and quieter than Emily."

Camilla half-smiled at the memory. It was true. She had never been boisterous. She had just wanted to escape.

"You would have been knocked up and living on welfare if it wasn't for me, you know," Theresa explained flatly. Camilla just sat and listened. She couldn't deny it. Theresa got up and walked around the room. "What a shithole North Carolina is. You're so lucky I got you out of there. Made you what you are."

Camilla nodded. All true.

"Do you think you're a better witch than me?" Theresa turned suddenly, the earlier fire and aggression back.

Camilla tensed but remained seated. She knew better than to get in a pissing match with Theresa.

"Do you? After five years you think you've learned what it takes to be a powerful witch?" Theresa stormed over to within inches of Camilla's face. Camilla was slightly confused. Where was all this coming from?

"I *will* kill Shane and I will make it my life's mission to destroy as many vampires as I can," Theresa continued. Her lips were speckled with spittle and her eyes were wild, matching her unruly hair and maniacal face.

So this was about loyalty.

"And I will be at your side as you do," Camilla said calmly, her voice steady as a beating drum.

This calmed Theresa somewhat. She backed away from her aggressive stance in Camilla's face. "You'd better be. If a handsome face can easily pull you from someone who *saved* your life, then you'll never make it as a witch."

"I'm grateful for all that you've done for me, Theresa." Camilla stood to match her coven leader. She knew she had to tread lightly, but she still couldn't shake the feeling of pity for Theresa. While Shane was kissing Camilla with abandon, Theresa's husband was leaving her.

"I had wanted to side with him. Did you know that? I offered to work with him." Theresa creased her forehead with the memory. "He declined. And I got stuck siding with that despicable betrayer. I hate that guy."

Camilla knew what Theresa was trying to say. At the end of the day, it was all unraveling. With a comforting hand on Theresa's shoulder, she said, "Let's go back to the salon. The girls are probably upset over the loss of Elyse."

Theresa reached out and touched Camilla's hair. "I always knew you'd be a beautiful poisonous flower. I raised you that way."

"There's still time. Let's go back to the salon," Camilla prodded.

"And Shane will come for you. His poisonous flower. Your seductive beauty so much more powerful than spells and incantation. Why did I not think of dangling *you* instead of Julianna?" Theresa spoke barely above a whisper, as if her thoughts were barely escaping as words from her lips.

Camilla swallowed hard. "Let's go."

But neither of them moved.

"Shane will come to save you, thinking you are his. And then we'll kill him. And you masterminded the whole thing." Theresa's eyes lit with the dawning of the perfect trap. "I have trained you so well." Theresa hugged Camilla again and Camilla hugged back, grateful to have the calm, proud Theresa and not the loose cannon of earlier. Theresa whispered in her ear. "When the time comes, *you* will kill Shane."

Camilla pulled back and Theresa tucked a strand of Camilla's loose hair behind her ear in a very motherly gesture. Camilla saw nothing but sincerity on Theresa's face, so she knew she now had her marching orders.

She was to kill the very man who had come to love her and trust her so completely.

"We should get back to the salon now, Theresa. The other witches need you." Camilla grabbed her hand and tugged.

Theresa finally seemed to get past her obsession with Shane and her anger at all the things that had gone awry. As the new plan became fleshed out in her mind, the one Camilla had really set into place, Theresa became more confident. More back on top. More in-control. She nodded at her young pretty witch, and they transported out of Theresa's beach house and instantly arrived in the middle of the warehouse.

And the witches there *did* need their coven leader. It was clear that things were beginning to fall apart.

10

Dawn was rising on another day. The sky was still dark enough to not burn their skin, but light enough that they could see the swirl of pinks and purples lightening the midnight blue. A cool morning breeze passed by every few minutes and a cricket played a soothing rhythm somewhere in the distance.

Isabelle stood next to the chair where Kara was sitting. She was ready for a fight, as always, but there was a new tension surrounding her. A small woodland animal would probably meet its end if it appeared at this moment. Her hair was still pulled back in a long ponytail and she wore tight black clothing and thick black boots. She was everything Kara wanted to be. Tough. Brave. Protective.

"Why do you think your sister wants to kill you?" Isabelle asked.

"Because she's a witch," Kara shrugged, as if that was all the rationale needed. "I can't believe she would side with Theresa. It's so unlike her."

"Maybe Theresa forced her? I mean, after the battle in the Cascades, there's no way Theresa could deny what she was and what you'd become."

Kara looked off into the distance. A few days ago she'd looked like an escapee from an asylum, but now she looked like the cute teenager she was and now forever would stay. Her blonde hair was smooth and flat against her back. Her eyes were bright, her face and hands clean. She wore a white shirt and a miniskirt which suited her, although blood on a white shirt would really stand out if she let her bloodthirstiness reign supreme.

"I've thought about that, for sure. It's likely all my fault," Kara replied. "But why Theresa? I could see her being angry and confused at my turning, but did she have to turn to that witch?"

"Kara." Isabelle's voice was almost stern and she spoke her name like a command. "The reality of our existence is that while we are alive as vampires, our human lives are over. Forget Emily. Forget Theresa. We're your family now."

Kara turned at that and it seemed to placate her for the moment. She stood and was only an inch shorter than Isabelle. "Teach me to fight."

Isabelle laughed and crossed her arms. "You want to learn my skills?"

"I want to be a warrior," she announced.

Isabelle smirked but knew she would welcome the lessons. She was really starting to care for Kara as she would a little sister. And, more pragmatically, she knew Kara would one day make a fierce warrior. "Fine."

Isabelle grabbed Kara's shoulders and squared her off in front of her. "Now bend your knees a little and extend your claws."

Kara did as she was instructed.

"As a vampire, it is more important than ever that you draw first blood. So strike out, but strike to slice, not just bruise." Isabelle gestured for Kara to advance. "Now come at me."

Kara leapt from where she stood a foot in front of Isabelle, and she was fast, but Isabelle was faster. Kara had gone claws first and Isabelle stepped to the side, knocking Kara to the ground by hitting her as she flew past.

"You have to get to them before you can slice, though," Isabelle explained as Kara stood and got back into position. "Again."

This time Kara was able to move fast enough to at least get to Isabelle. She struck her chest, just as Isabelle grabbed her hand and twisted it so she flipped and landed on her back.

"That was better," Isabelle announced, beaming. "You actually touched me that time."

Kara stood quickly and decided to use the element of surprise to catch Isabelle off guard. Without pausing, she stood and rushed her mentor, grabbing her at her hips and knocking her to the ground. Both girls bounced as they fell, Isabelle laughing at Kara's success.

It was a tackle that surprised Isabelle, with Kara as the aggressor, that Shane and Luke saw when they walked out to the patio.

"The student has become the master, I see," Shane announced.

Laughing, Isabelle stood out from under Kara, brushing the dirt off her black jeans. "I wouldn't go that far, but she will be one day. She's better than you by a mile."

Kara smiled at the praise and Shane just shook his head. "I have no doubt that's true."

"Don't let Kara go thinking that's some kind of compliment," Luke laughed along with Isabelle. "Shane would have died his first night as a vampire if he hadn't learned to control fire. Which I taught him to do."

Luke was teasing, a playful gleam in his handsome eye, but Shane said in all seriousness, "Also true."

"Wait. Luke taught you to control fire?" Kara asked.

Shane and Luke exchanged a glance,

remembering that night in the Bellinz compound where Regina had kept them both as prisoners.

Shane answered Kara. "Well, he helped me to see the possibility."

Luke added, "All because Regina wanted to abuse us sexually. It isn't easy being this good-looking."

Isabelle rolled her eyes, but Shane chuckled at Luke's humor. His sarcastic, carefree soul is what Shane had liked about him from the beginning.

"You wanna try and take me down, Shane? For old times' sake?" Isabelle asked, bouncing on her knees, preparing for a sparring match.

"No, I'm not interested in an ass-beating today, Isabelle," Shane said, and then turned his attention to the younger vampire. "I came to find you, Kara."

"Me?" Kara asked.

Shane nodded. "You have a visitor on her way. She'll be here any minute."

A little hesitant, Kara asked, "Who is it?"

Isabelle crossed her arms, appearing like a bodyguard next to Kara. She was impulsive and aggressive, but she'd do anything to protect her family. She'd proven that when she'd taken the lightning bolt from Theresa in the Cascades.

"She doesn't know I know, so act surprised when your sister arrives," Shane instructed.

"How *do* you know?" Isabelle asked.

"My powers."

"Are they coming to kill me again?" Kara asked. There was no fear in her voice, just pure curiosity.

Shane shook his head. "No. I think all that might be over."

Kara looked at Isabelle, who said, "If they try anything, it'll be the last thing they do." Kara smiled at that. They really were two peas in a pod.

A waver in the air slowly turned into two witches materializing before them. One had dark hair and skin, the other blonde. When they fully appeared, the vampires quickly recognized Emily. Isabelle instinctively stood in front of Kara, blocking Emily's path should she try anything.

Not having any idea what she would encounter

when she appeared unannounced at a vampire compound, Emily sucked in a bit of air at the sight before her. She knew Shane was really powerful and Luke had turned her sister and Isabelle had kicked her in the chest earlier today.

Emily spoke first. "We're not here to fight."

It was Isabelle who answered. "Then why are you here?"

Shane folded his arms and stood with his legs in a wide stance. He wasn't as tall and broad as Luke, but standing like this he was still formidable. "She wants an alliance."

Emily was surprised at Shane's response, but only for a second. "Henna and I were sent by Theresa to find Julianna. We know where she is. But we don't want to hand her over to Theresa."

"Because?" Luke prodded.

Emily swallowed hard as she looked at Luke. Handsome as he was, she could only see the monster that took her sister from her. But she tried to think past that, knowing this was bigger than she was. "Theresa has lost it. She tried to kill me earlier and all she wants to do is kill vampires. We don't want to work with the betrayer anymore and our coven is slowly falling apart thanks to her fixations."

"Why the hell did you side with her in the first place, Emily?" Kara's hands were on her hips as she stared down her sister.

"I was angry and I knee-jerk reacted. I had wanted revenge too for what *he* did to you in the mountains," Emily pointed at Luke, who just raised an eyebrow in response. "But seeing Theresa today, the *real* Theresa, I know I made a big mistake."

"You tried to kill me just a few hours ago!" Kara shouted at her sister.

"We were trying to *save* you," Emily responded.

"By killing me?"

"Yes."

Henna spoke for the first time, her voice calm, her classy demeanor diffusing the situation. "When Julianna was resurrected, she came back as a human."

"What?" Isabelle whispered completely in

shock.

Shane looked at Luke and then turned back to the witches. "I can tell you are telling the truth."

Emily stepped forward, trying to get a better look at her sister around Isabelle. "So if you come with me, Henna and I can resurrect you and return you to being human." Emily was beaming, as if she was offering the most glorious prize.

But Kara recoiled, her face filled with revulsion. Not the reaction Emily had expected. Not by a mile. "I don't want to be a human!" Kara shook her head. "I'm a vampire—a good vampire."

Emily stepped forward again, her eyes pleading. "But then you can come home and live with me and dad again."

Kara took a step back in response to her sister's step toward her. "This is my family now. I don't want to go back to that existence."

"Oh." Emily let everything sink in. Before her stood a girl she'd once known, who was now a monster. Maybe there was no reasoning with a monster, especially if that monster enjoyed being what they were. "Why would you want to kill people, Kara?"

"What do you think witches do, Emily? What do you think Theresa did to our mom?" Kara spat back. "Don't come here trying to save me only to turn me into your type of evil instead of mine."

"Emily," Shane stepped toward her, hands up to show he meant no aggression. "Kara doesn't want to be turned back, but that doesn't mean you can't have a relationship. We welcome witches here. You can stay with us. We'll protect you from Theresa."

"Live with vampires?" Henna asked, as if the thought had never occurred to her and still seemed too far-fetched to be an actual option.

"Yes. Camilla lives here completely freely," Shane explained.

"And we all know how well that turned out." Isabelle rolled her eyes.

"She'll be back as soon as I go save her," Shane stated.

"The only way you'll get Camilla back is if

Theresa is dead. She's Theresa's protégé," Emily stated.

"See? Camilla can't be trusted," Isabelle said to Shane.

"Then again, I was her protégé too, and yet here I am," Emily explained.

"Kinda proving the point," Isabelle responded.

"We don't want to fight witches," Henna stepped forward. "We'll help you find Julianna, but that's it."

"And we'd never ask you to," Shane nodded at Henna. "Believe it or not, we're trying to live a peaceful existence here."

"But why did you kidnap me and my sister?" Emily had to ask Shane. He stood there now in solidarity with her, and, true, he seemed kindhearted, but a few weeks ago he was ready to kill them both.

"I needed leverage against Theresa. I needed something to make her back down." Shane's face softened. "I'm sorry I used you. But I am not sorry about Kara. She's like a sister to me now and I wouldn't want to change that."

As he said the words, he knew now they were

true. And then it made everything Julianna had done for him make complete sense. She had never thought of the fact she was taking his old life; she was focused on the life she was giving him. And she had probably loved to share her second life with him. He had loved it. And human or vampire, he would do whatever he could to protect Julianna now. He almost had her back. Again.

"You are both welcome to stay here. No harm will come to you. I'll have Elias protect you while I am gone," Shane explained to Henna and Emily. "But I need to know where Julianna is, so I can save her before I go save Camilla and kill Theresa."

"I'm killing Theresa," Kara reminded him.

"She's with the betrayer," Emily stated, looking sideways at her sister, slightly appalled at her bloodthirstiness. But she understood the sentiment. Theresa had ruined their lives.

"Dimas, that fucker," Luke muttered.

"They're barely even hiding. He took Julianna to Beck's. It's a bar like two doors down from Theresa's salon, where the coven is," Emily finished explaining.

"Thank you." Shane rested a gentle hand on Emily's shoulder, and she was surprised it didn't make her flinch. Had she already forgiven him? So easily? "Could he possibly have left when the bar closed?"

It was Henna who chimed in. "We ran a locator spell moments ago and they were still there. Probably hiding somewhere to stay indoors when the sun rises. And he knows a bar won't open at eight in the morning."

Shane turned to his team. "I don't want to lose the day, so I'll go alone. The sun is already coming up."

"Bullshit," Luke responded. "I love you, Shane, but you're not confronting Dimas without me."

"We can't wait for nightfall, Luke. That means Julianna is with Dimas as a *human* unprotected for a full day." Shane was remorseful, but he couldn't risk Luke's or Julianna's safety. "I'm the only one who can walk in the sunlight."

Emily swallowed hard. She still didn't like Luke much, but she wanted this to end, so she said, "He can wear my cloak." She unclasped the neck and swung it around her shoulders. "With the hood up, the sunlight won't touch your skin unless you look up."

She reached out in offering, and Luke took it with a debonair smile. "Hey, thanks. That's perfect."

"Thank you, Emily. That's genius," Shane said warmly. Then he turned to Luke, Isabelle and Kara. "So Luke and I will go get Julianna. You two get indoors before the sun comes up and we'll regroup later and attack Theresa tonight."

Isabelle stepped forward and looked straight at Shane, her annoyance plain on her face. "Shane, when are you going to learn? These bitches better come up with two more cloaks, because we're coming too. Two doors down from the salon? We get Julianna, we kill Dimas and then we go kill Theresa. Boom. We're not waiting for nightfall. We'll have the element of surprise on *our* side for once."

Smiling at Isabelle's ferocity, Shane turned back to Henna and Emily. "Can you ladies get two more cloaks for Isabelle and Kara?"

Henna nodded, "We can."

But Emily looked at Kara with frightened eyes.

"Does Kara have to go?"

Kara looked at Emily with the softest face she'd shown since her resurrection a couple nights prior. "Don't worry about me. I'm tougher than I look. And I want to be there when Theresa dies."

Shane vouched for Kara, gesturing to her with his thumb. "Seriously. This girl is one tough vampire."

Emily reached forward and pulled her sister into a hug. Kara, caught off guard, patted her sister's back awkwardly but didn't pull away. She could smell her sister's blood and hear the rhythmic thumping of her heart. She awkwardly resisted drinking her own sister's blood. When Emily finished the embrace, she smoothed her sister's hair back. "When I saw you...bitten, that night in the mountains, I thought I'd never see you again. And then Theresa told me you were a monster, and I believed her. But all I see right now is my baby sister." Emily turned to Shane with a sad smile. "She's always been tough."

"Emily," Kara called to her sister, and her sister turned back to her. "I'm getting back at her for mom."

Emily nodded wordlessly at her sister.

"Give us five minutes to get the cloaks," Henna chimed in.

"We'll be waiting inside. And thank you for your alliance. I know it took a lot of courage to come here," Shane said to the witches.

There was a nervous anticipation in the air. Luke actually bounced on the balls of his feet. "Dimas dies today. If that's not justice, I don't know what is."

"We have to remember Julianna could be in a very fragile state. I may need you, Isabelle and Kara, to help her out of there while I help Luke kill Dimas," Shane said to his vampire family.

Isabelle nodded, affirming she would carry out her orders like the good soldier she was. While it would be fun to kill Dimas, she didn't have the burning need that Luke did and she was well aware of that fact.

"We'll get Julianna somewhere safely and then surprise Theresa. She won't expect a daytime attack. But I don't want to kill any more witches than we have to, so focus on immobilizing, not killing," Shane instructed. All the vampires nodded solemnly in response, a little bummed at the desire not to kill.

"We'll be back," Henna stated and grabbed Emily's arm as they began to transport to go get the additional cloaks.

But before the witches completely dematerialized, Shane heard Emily say, "Shane. Watch your back with Camilla."

Isabelle couldn't agree more, but she said nothing. She knew the heart didn't always listen to the brain. She looked at Shane and his face remained impassive. If he worried about the words of warning, he didn't let it show.

When Shane and Luke turned back toward the compound, Isabelle and Kara followed. The sun was just beginning to pierce the sky in between the mountain tops in the distance. A new day was dawning, signaling their next battle.

And nothing energized Isabelle as much as an impending attack. She let her fangs extend as she steeled her body for the coming fight. This was going to be a bloody day. Hearts would be ripped out, witches beheaded, arms torn off. And Isabelle smiled wickedly at the thought.

Vengeance was coming. And she was a bitch.

11

In the darkest corner of Beck's, an unassuming bar near the Ventura pier, a disgruntled vampire and a frightened vampire-turned-human waited quietly. Toward the front they could see the daylight beginning to trickle through the windows and doors. The Beck's staff had long since gone home and no one would be here for hours.

Julianna and Dimas had said very few words in the hours they'd been waiting in here. With the exception of one curious young man, they had remained hidden to all, customers and staff alike. Dimas had taken care of that young man easily enough, compelling him forward until he could sink his fangs into the young man's neck. Julianna covered her mouth at the sight, but she didn't want to scream. She was afraid of what might happen if she tried to escape or if someone tried to help her. They'd be sucked dry just like this guy was. Dimas hid the victim's body behind some boxes in a storage closet. They would find his shriveled up remains soon enough, but Dimas didn't care. He and his prize would be long gone by then.

"So what happens now?" Julianna dared to ask as she watched the dust particles float in the early morning light.

"We wait," Dimas answered without looking at Julianna. "You might not turn for a few days. And even then, I don't know what those witches did to you. You should be dead right now, waiting for rebirth as a vampire."

Julianna didn't want to tell him that she didn't think the blood he had forced down her throat was going to work. Let her have a few more days of waiting. It was what followed those few days that Julianna dreaded. When she didn't turn into a vampire, what would he do to her? What would he do to everyone around him?

"I had wanted you to be my bride, did you know that? To rule the Strashni by my side," Dimas said in a defeated voice.

"I would've married you at one time, willingly, too," Julianna said, knowing it was true even if it now disgusted her.

"Maybe you'll remember how you loved me when you're a vampire again."

"Are we going to wait here?" Julianna asked. She glanced nervously at the closet to her right where the young man's body was stored. She didn't want to stay trapped between a monster and a dead body for days.

Dimas turned back to Julianna angrily. "Do you have a better idea?"

The truth was, Dimas had nowhere to go. The last few centuries had been spent at the Strashni compound, but there was no way he was bringing Julianna back near her brother and Luke, even if he could find a pocket of the compound to hide in quietly enough. If he was going to keep her for himself, he would need to get her far from here. Europe, perhaps? As soon as she was a vampire again, they would head toward Canada. At least they'd be far from these tribes and these covens. They could figure out their next move from there. He hadn't been one to make alliances over the years, but he did know a few vampires in the East he could possibly connect with.

Dimas turned back toward the front of the bar, wallowing in his self-pity. It was fitting that he was feeling this way in a bar. He walked to where the glasses were kept and grabbed a bottle of whiskey from the shelf. He poured and drank it straight with no blood. He could have used Julianna's, but he still wasn't sure how tainted she was by what the witches had done. So he drowned his sorrows with straight whiskey, even though as a vampire he would never get drunk.

"Want some?" Dimas offered to Julianna. She shook her head but said nothing. She looked different to him somehow. Scared. Mousey. Pathetic little human. He missed the bold vampire she'd been. If she didn't turn in a few days, he'd have to kill her again. He wasn't going to deal with this disgrace for much longer.

He poured another glass of whiskey and went back to the job of feeling sorry for himself. His beautiful plan to take over all vampires with the prophecy and use the witches had backfired. And it was all Shane's fault. And Theresa's. Why had he ever thought it was a good idea to bring her into all this? She'd made it worse from the start. And then they brainwashed Julianna to think *they* were her saviors? And to add insult to injury they blocked his dream of turning Julianna back into a vampire so they could be together for eternity. They thought of her as one of them? Disgusting.

He slammed the glass down with a thud, forcefully punctuating his frustration with the events that had transpired. Julianna jumped and stepped back from him.

She looked at Dimas differently now too. He had been her mentor, her hero, like an older brother to her. Now she saw his stringy white hair and crumpled clothes as a symbol of his disgraced coup. He had overreached and this is what had come of it. She didn't trust him. And even more, she was finding that she didn't even like him. And his new big plan was to turn her back into a monster and kidnap her? How had she ever been so blind to his true nature?

And worse still, she knew it wouldn't be good when he discovered in a few days that she wasn't a vampire. He had forced his blood down her throat, but he'd have to kill her again. And yet, he couldn't kill her again because of the witches' spell. And she felt nothing but nauseous over the whole thing. There was no part of her that felt the turn of becoming a vampire. She knew—she'd done it once before.

For a moment, he stared at her and she stared at him, both with frustration plain on their faces.

Then Dimas lifted his shot glass and took another swallow of whiskey.

Something deep in Julianna's core told her that she was a trapped mouse, and like a trapped animal she had to escape or die. In a split second she made the decision to run. It wasn't something she thought through, just acted on impulse. She thought of escape and so bolted for the front windows. She had thankfully made it to the area where sunlight was pouring through and she knew he couldn't follow, but Dimas had effortlessly caught up with her and grabbed her arm, pulling her back into the shadows.

His hand had singed a bit in the sunlight as he'd reached out to grab her, but he didn't even grimace. Anger overpowered the burning pain. Julianna watched the smoldering flesh but turned worried eyes to Dimas. His eyes were those of a demon. Solid black, filled with pure hatred. He was way beyond frustrated or angry now. He looked ready to kill.

He picked her up and threw her against the bar. She'd have gone unconscious if he'd been a strong vampire. As it was, she felt bruised from head to toe with a possible concussion. Still, her determination to get away from Dimas was stronger than her pain, so she scrambled back to her feet and ran back toward the front windows. But he caught her easily. It was no use. Her human form was no match for his vampire abilities.

As he extended his claws and raised his arm to

strike the final blow to the human before him, Julianna realized that all she could feel was a sense of relief. A swift death was better than waiting for days in the clutches of the betrayer—or becoming his vampire bride. She squeezed her eyes shut, preparing for his strike.

But what came instead was a loud crash of glass shattering behind her. Had Dimas missed his mark that badly? Curiosity overcame her and she turned to see Shane standing in the sunlight, lit from head to toe and not a single reaction to the light touching his skin. Behind him stood what appeared to be three witches, covered by black robes.

"Shane," she murmured in shock. It was in that instant that she knew beyond a shadow of a doubt that her brother had been the chosen one from the prophecy, just as she'd always believed. Memories came flooding back to her like a wave crashing on the shore. It was almost too much at once and they overwhelmed her. Becoming a Strashni. Fighting for their lands. Pledging loyalty to Dimas. Hearing the prophecy, knowing it was her brother. Killing her brother. Resurrecting her brother. Falling in love with Luke. Dying at Dimas' hands.

Dimas acted quickly and pulled her in front of him just as she was realizing her human instincts about the man were better than her vampire ones. She tried to reach for the light. The sunlight called to her like a life jacket thrown to someone lost at sea. It was her salvation. If she could just get to the light, she would be free. Only her brother was a vampire who could walk in the light. Dimas had no power over her there. He pulled her back into the shadows, but she kept reaching with every limb.

The precious light. It was right there.

"This feels a lot like déjà vu," Dimas sneered, clutching Julianna with all his might, his claws digging into her skin and leaving blood trails where it pierced. Julianna felt it but remained focused on her futile effort to get to the light.

Shane stepped into the bar, leaving the precious sunlight behind. Julianna felt insane because she could swear that even as he stepped into the shadows, sunlight danced upon his hair, making it almost like a halo. She stopped squirming and remembered that this *was* déjà vu. Dimas had done this before.

"You'd like to think that, I'm sure, you piece of shit." Shane swiped his arm at the air in front of him and Julianna felt Dimas' hold break free, even as he howled in her ear. She turned around to see both his arms seared off at the wrists, burnt and charred at the ends, his wrists severed from the stumps. Julianna stared dumbfoundedly. Shane had freed her without laying a finger on Dimas.

Dimas fell to his knees screaming as he stared at what remained of his arms. Julianna took a step back.

One of the witches came forward into the shadows and removed the hood of their cloak. Julianna and Dimas were both surprised that the witch wasn't a witch at all, but was Luke.

Shane, calm as he always was, spoke smoothly, standing before Dimas with his arms folded. A finger flick and Dimas would be dead, burnt to a crisp. But it was like a German shepherd around a poodle—the big dog has no need to prove his dominance. It's just there. "I would love the honor of killing the great betrayer, but you see, I already promised that honor to Luke."

As Luke removed his cloak, two of the other vampires dressed as witches came forward and pulled Julianna back toward the shattered glass at the front of the bar. She went willingly toward the safety of the sunlight. As much as she might have wondered who was pulling on her, she kept her eyes riveted on Luke's tall, muscular form standing over Dimas' cowering puddle on the floor.

Dimas made a small showing of baring his fangs, but what else could he do to protect himself? Luke walked easily behind Dimas in two long strides and before Dimas could react, Luke had twisted his neck and cleanly removed his head from his body. The whole thing was over in an instant. Dimas' lifeless body, arm stumps and all, fell with a thud to the concrete bar floor. Blood spilled out of Dimas' neck, pooling like red paint.

"Burn his body, but I say we keep his head and

put it on a spike back home," Luke said. His typical smirk was back, as if a huge burden had suddenly lifted from his shoulders. And Julianna felt it too. Her nightmare had ended.

From next to Julianna, a woman's voice yelled, "Hell, yeah!"

She turned to see Isabelle, the one she remembered as a warrior vampire, under the dark hood.

"Fine," Shane said and flicked his wrist toward Dimas' severed neck and body. It went up in flames, burning out in a minute and leaving behind a pile of ash. Then he flicked toward the two severed arms, which also burned to a crisp. Even the pool of blood had evaporated from the flames. No one would ever deny something had happened there, but the humans that might come along later would never be able to guess.

"In the closet," Julianna stammered, her heart pounding in her chest from the night and morning's ordeal. Shane turned toward his sister. "Dimas killed him, drank his blood. His...body is in the closet." She shivered at the thought. Her human frailty was so apparent.

Shane nodded, knowing exactly what to do.

As Shane headed to the closet to dispose of Dimas' victim, Luke walked tentatively toward Julianna. He wanted to sweep her up into his arms, but he carried Dimas' head in one hand and her eyes kept darting nervously to it, and he was afraid she still blamed him for her previous demise.

About a foot in front of her, Luke stopped. "It was all Dimas. I would never hurt you."

There was so much hurt on his face, she knew the accusation was burrowing deep into his soul. She stepped forward to meet him and placed a hand gently on his cheek. He welcomed the touch. "I know, Luke. My memories are starting to come back. I remember that day. Dimas betrayed us all."

In response, Luke sucked in a deep breath through his nose. He smelled the intoxicating scent of human flesh and blood. "So it's true then? You're human again?"

"Yes. I don't know if it's something the witches did or what, but when I resurrected the second time, I was human again. Plain ole Julianna Walker."

"You could never be plain," Luke said to her. He touched his forehead to hers. "Will you forgive me?"

"There's nothing to forgive," Julianna said, embracing his arms. "I've loved you from the moment I met you."

"I hate to break up this little rendezvous, but people walking by are starting to notice the broken glass, and they'll be sure to notice the severed head you're carrying." Isabelle's voice came from behind Julianna. "Can we go kill some witches now?"

Shane came out from the closet area and took command. He looked ready for battle, all dressed in black, a stunning contrast to his blonde curly hair. "Yeah, let's go. We've done what we came to do at Beck's."

Looking all around, Luke added, "And then some. I have a sneaking suspicion there will be a lot of unanswered questions when the police arrive."

"What do you mean, kill witches?" Julianna asked. A part of her had always been uncomfortable amongst them, but part of her was grateful they had saved her life. She certainly did not think they deserved to die.

Isabelle rolled her eyes, "Okay, okay. Kill one witch and just wound the others."

Shane put his hand up indicating that Isabelle should let him do the explaining. "This tit for tat that Dimas instigated with the witches will never end until Theresa is dead. We don't want to kill all the witches, but we want to move forward in peace."

"Theresa saved my life from Dimas," Julianna explained.

"Then she intended to use you to some purpose." Kara stepped forward, lifting her head under the hood to reveal herself for the first time. "She takes a life as easily as she saves it, believe me. We're not martyring a saint."

"Who are you?" Julianna turned to Shane. "She's just a child."

"I'm fourteen, thank you very much," Kara responded, hands on her hips. "And Theresa killed my mother."

Shane just shook his head. "Don't underestimate Kara, Julianna. She's tougher than she looks. And this is personal for all of us." Walking toward Julianna, Shane pulled her into an embrace. "And I'm glad you're alive, in any form. I really missed you."

Julianna fought uselessly to hide a smile. "I missed you too, squirt."

"Squirt? Do I even want to know?" Isabelle asked.

"Childhood nickname," Julianna explained.

"It's not so bad. Mine was Licky," Luke chimed in.

Isabelle held up a hand. "Okay, I do NOT want to know."

"Mine was Care Bear," Kara added.

"Oh, that one is actually cute." Luke winked at her.

"Can we please go now? I seriously love that

Dimas is dead," Isabelle said, "but I'm here for witch blood."

"Julianna, you don't have to go in the salon if you don't want to." Shane looked protectively at his sister. Suddenly, their roles were reversed and the fragile human before him needed *his* protection.

Julianna looked up at Luke. "No, I'll come with you. I'm not afraid."

"I won't let anything happen to her," Luke told Shane. Shane nodded because he knew truer words were never spoken. Luke would die before he lost Julianna again.

"What are you going to do with that?" Shane asked, gesturing toward Dimas' head dangling from Luke's arm.

"Oh, this? I'll be walking in and holding it up high. Show those bitches what happens to people who betray the Dark Prophecy." Luke held the head high for effect, Dimas' blood dripping down his hand and arm. Only Julianna frowned at the sight.

"Perfect.   Sounds   like   a   plan,"   Isabelle

responded. To Shane, she said, "Lead the way, fearless leader."

Shane stepped forward, back into the sunlight as if he were any typical man on the planet and not the leader of a bunch of vampires. Luke, Isabelle and Kara pulled up their hoods and followed him. Julianna watched with human eyes and shook her head. There was no way this would go unnoticed in Ventura harbor.

She stepped into the sunlight and turned her face upward, taking only a moment to enjoy the light on her face. It had been years since she had felt this free. Whatever happened from here on out, she was going to enjoy her second life—this gift she'd been given. Her memories told her that her vampire life had been a good one. Happy. But she was overjoyed to be human again. To be able to lay out on the beach, soaking in the sun. To eat pizza. Even being weak and slow held more meaning for her than she'd ever considered. She was comfortable with not being a predator anymore.

Her brother, dressed in military-style garb, and three hooded figures marched down the street toward

Theresa's salon. Julianna raced to catch up. Even as a human with sketchy memories she knew it was time.

It was time to end this.

12

Emily paced the floor of the compound where she and Henna had been left in Elias' care. Oddly, her nervousness had nothing to do with being in a house full of vampires. For someone betraying her own kind, Henna sat comfortably on the large sectional that filled the family room which connected to the kitchen. There were large windows with the shades drawn, but enough that Emily could see this was a beautiful room. Everything was classical, retro, but tastefully decorated.

"You're making me anxious. Sit down," Elias instructed as he watched Emily wander the room. He sat back, one foot resting on the other knee, his long dark hair pulled back. Emily studied him. He was fierce-looking. Tall and lean. Intimidating. In another life, she might have cried at his nearness.

Instead, she sighed. "I can't. I feel so guilty." Her fingers twisted together, protruding out at odd angles.

Elias stretched his long arms across the back of the sectional. "Guilty? It's Theresa who should feel guilty. And Dimas. They've created a battle that didn't need to exist. We've lived among witches for centuries."

"It had to be done, Emily," Henna said simply. Her legs were crossed at the ankles and she was poised as always. Her calm demeanor slightly eased Emily's nerves, but not by much. "I've regenerated a few times, so I've seen a thing or two. And Elias is right. We can live the way we want to peacefully. It is possible to co-exist."

"She's my stepmother," Emily said with a frown.

"Because she contrived it," Henna explained.

Emily didn't really care about Theresa; it had all been revenge from the start. Her emotions had changed her. She had no response, so she turned to Elias, "Why is my sister so in love with being a vampire?"

Elias huffed a laugh. "She's *your* sister. You never saw how naturally aggressive she was?"

Emily shook her head. "It's all my fault. I should have protected Kara. Now she's fighting Theresa and it's because I betrayed her. I'm no better than Dimas."

At this Elias stood up. "It's not betrayal to turn in a criminal. It's justice. Dimas was backstabbing everyone and lying about the prophecy for his own gain. You are saving hundreds of vampires and witches alike. Wallow in self-pity if you must, but move past it soon. It will get old."

Emily looked up and saw that though his face was stern, his eyes were soft. It was good advice he gave. Her shoulders slumped a little as his words sank in.

Henna stood up to join Elias and Emily. She rested a gentle hand on Emily's shoulder. "Theresa is more than a witch. She's controlling and evil, power-hungry. You'll see when she's gone and you can practice your craft freely, just as I did before I met her. *She* made it evil. I've been wanting to bring her down for decades, but there was no way to do it on my own. I'm at peace because I know this is the right thing to do."

Emily thought about this. Did she really feel guilty about handing Theresa over to the vampires? Not really. She'd never had any real love for her stepmother. What was really bothering her?

"I'll be happy when Theresa is gone." Emily knew the words were true the second they left her lips.

"Me too," Henna smiled. "So why so upset, Emily?"

"Because I'm a coward," Emily stated with a frown. "I've always been. While Kara is tough and strong, I'm just a coward." She turned to look up to Elias. "But I don't want to be anymore. I should be there."

Elias wrinkled his brow. "Shane told me to keep you safe."

Emily laid a hand on his arm. "I understand if you don't want to come, but I am going to that salon. I need to look Theresa in the eye. I shouldn't tattle and hide. I should stand in the circle and point her out."

"Shane can move the earth and form fire out of the thin air. He is the only one who can handle Theresa," Elias said. "But if you feel you should be there, then as your sworn protector, I am coming too." Elias flashed a wicked grin, fangs beginning to extend. "Shane told me to watch over you."

Emily smiled and looked back at Henna. "Wanna come?"

The first look of worry Emily had seen all day crossed Henna's face. "The other witches will never forgive us."

"Or they'll thank us," Emily responded, giving Henna's hand a squeeze. "As you said, we're doing the right thing."

"Let's go. We don't want to miss anything." Elias spoke impassively, but there was a wicked delight in his eye. Babysitting wasn't his passion, but fighting, protecting, and killing was. He turned and started for the garage. He could run at vampire speed, but he knew the witches couldn't.

"Elias? Where are you going?" Emily asked.

"I might be a vampire, but I can still ride in style. There's a Ferrari in the garage and I drive *fast*," Elias raised an eyebrow.

Henna pushed up her sleeves. "As much as I'd love to watch you drive like a maniac, nothing is faster than instantaneous."

Emily waived Elias over. "We have teleportation spells. Just hold my hand and Henna's spell will cover all of us."

"Is it safe to use on a vampire?" Elias asked, slightly nervous. He didn't know the witches *that* well.

Henna looked at him sideways. "Really? I've had all day to kill you but I wait until we're going to surprise attack my leader?"

"It doesn't really matter if you are human, vampire, animal, thing...the spell just transports what it covers. Witchcraft doesn't play favorites, the witches do," Emily explained.

"And anyway, I've started to grow fond of your vampire brooding," Henna said with a teasing smile.

Elias shook his head. "All right, all right.

Teleport me."

Henna looked at Emily and then Elias, rolling her shoulders back. "Are we ready?"

Emily looked up at Elias who nodded back to her. She replied to Henna. "We're ready."

"Let's go witness Theresa's demise," Henna stated. She was a great witch, so she hid her emotions well. Emily saw none of the nervousness from before. There was no excitement or sadness either. Just statement of fact.

And with a wave of Henna's hands, Elias, Emily and Henna shimmered and faded from sight. In a moment they were gone from the vampire compound and standing in the back warehouse of Theresa's salon.

13

Theresa was almost insane with anger.

The morning sun was creeping through the high windows at the top of the warehouse. She stood before the Harbor Coven of witches, barely keeping herself together. Hot, fuming breaths came barreling out of her nose in great huffs.

She had built this coven from the ground up. They owed everything to her. And yet they were useless without her. Apparently, they couldn't do anything without her.

And the witches of the Harbor Coven stared back at her. Some were nervous, fearful of Theresa's wrath. Others were disappointed in her behavior. All stayed quiet and watched Theresa pace and fume. Her hair was no longer perfectly pulled back in its usual bun. Her normally perfectly pressed professional clothes were wrinkled and untucked. The woman who had taught them all to be poised and never let emotions show was sure not the woman yelling at them now.

But Camilla stood at her side and she *was* perfectly poised. Her brown hair pulled low on her shoulder, but smooth. Her hands folded neatly in front of her. Her face was impassive and calm. The harbor coven needed a leader and it was looking more and more like Camilla would be that person.

"I leave you for a few minutes and you lose Julianna and Dimas escapes!" Theresa screamed. "And now Henna and Emily are missing! Elyse is dead!"

She ran her fingers through her messy hair, and it went even wilder, matching her eyes and demeanor.

One of the older witches, named Collette, stepped forward. She was normally very quiet, but Theresa's behavior was shocking her enough to embolden her. "Theresa, you can't possibly blame us for any of this. You are the one who started a war with vampires."

Theresa turned wild eyes on Collette, seemingly laser-focused on the woman who dare speak up. Apparently, she was going to have to be teaching some lessons today. Some witches were forgetting their place. "How dare you! I've done nothing but bring this coven to greatness." Theresa reached out and from a few feet away, lifted Collette off the ground with the force of her power, holding her up by her neck without touching her. Collette's feet dangled beneath her. Theresa was almost getting tired of having to use this move to teach witches lessons.

Collette might look like she was twenty-five, but she was a century older than that and quite an experienced witch. And she was angry too. She had been happy with their coven. All the politics of late had unraveled everything they had built. She pushed the air in front of her and Theresa slid back across the floor, falling backward.

And when Theresa fell, Collette also fell back to the floor, landing in a heap. Most of the witches gasped and stepped back, lest they be the next victim.

Theresa stood up and slowly lifted her arms, anger rolling off of her in waves. Collette knew retaliation was imminent, so she scrambled to her feet as well, but Theresa got her spell off while Collette was still trying to get her balance. With a push of her hands, Theresa sent Collette flying backwards, cartwheeling through the air and landing in a heap on top of cardboard boxes in the back of the warehouse. The same boxes Dimas had used a day ago as his makeshift throne.

Collette felt a piercing pain shooting through her leg and looked down to see bone protruding through skin just under her knee. A breath and she realized Theresa had also broken one of her ribs. Thanks to the rejuvenation spell, Collette was able to easily pop her bones back in and begin to heal, but the pain was still there. She sucked it up because Theresa was marching toward her with the devil in her eyes.

Collette prepared to go on the offensive with another spell, hoping to get it off before Theresa did, but

Camilla stepped in front of Theresa, both shocking her and stopping her in her tracks.

"Enough," Camilla stated flatly. "We need to focus. There's an enemy out there and it's not each other."

Theresa glared at Camilla and then turned her attention to Collette, still sitting there amongst a sea of boxes. "You try anything else and you're a dead witch."

Collette rolled her eyes and stood up. She agreed with Camilla that the fighting was unnecessary, but she was tired of putting up with Theresa. "Give it up, Theresa. After centuries of using witchcraft to put yourself on top, you screwed up. It's over."

Theresa's shoulders heaved and her urge to kill Collette was overwhelming, but Camilla looked in her eyes and begged her for peace. Theresa backed down, but she made a mental note that it was only for now. There would be plenty of time to kill Collette later.

"Pull yourself together, Theresa," Camilla whispered so the other witches wouldn't hear. "This isn't you."

Except that Camilla didn't know how very much it *was* Theresa. Theresa had to exercise incredible restraint and control in order to keep her usual demeanor. Inside, the volcano had been building for years. And Elyse's death was the final event that pushed everything over the edge.

First her precious Kara, the stepdaughter who was born to be a witch. And they'd stolen her from her. Then Dimas steals her collateral, that scheming two-faced bastard. And finally, the loss of Elyse. Her number two. The witch she'd loved as a sister. The pain was blinding her, the loss of control of the situation creating a fissure in her barely-put-together façade.

Theresa's eyes flicked toward the other witches who were watching everything in complete horror. This definitely wasn't the look she wanted to see reflected back at her from her coven. The coven *she* had created, she reminded herself. Theresa stood up straight and took a moment to try and smooth out her hair and then wiped down her skirt, although it didn't help. She still looked awful.

"Camilla is right," Theresa spoke loudly, trying to capture her old sense of self. "I am very upset over the loss of Elyse. She was a beautiful witch who was murdered by those monsters. We need to find Julianna before Dimas turns her. And we need to find Henna and Emily before something happens to them."

A rustle near the boxes alerted the witches' attention to where Collette had fallen. Only now she was in the air again, and Theresa hadn't done it. A flame shot up into the air and stopped inches from Collette's throat, like a flaming spear. Collette's eyes widened in shock and fear and she instinctively pulled her neck away from the flame, but her body was held tight even as she dangled in the air.

"Beautiful speech. Very moving, Theresa." Shane walked out from behind the boxes, his arm pointed up at Collette.

Theresa's nostrils flared at the sight. Her barely calm demeanor was gone again in a second. Theresa watched as three witches in long black hooded cloaks walked in behind him. Who had he teamed up with now?

"If you are here for Julianna, I don't have her anymore. The betrayer took her. Go see him." Theresa waved at Shane and tried to pretend that Shane's entrance didn't bother her. The Harbor Coven watched on, trying to take their direction from Theresa and Camilla. They tensed, preparing for a fight.

A fight that *she* had brought on them and that they were all tired of.

Camilla stared right at Shane, who glanced at her only momentarily. She kept her face completely impassive. If she was scared or worried about her betrayal and what he might do to her for it, it didn't show at all.

"Oh, I know. We've already killed him." Shane stepped toward the witches. Julianna stepped into the warehouse behind Shane and the three people in black cloaks. There were gasps and some sighs of relief from the Harbor Coven.

"Come back to us, Julianna," Theresa coaxed. "Shane will want to turn you back into a vampire."

"I'm not here to turn anyone into anything. And I don't want to hurt any of you if I don't have to." He looked over at the witches, carefully avoiding eye contract with Theresa. "I'm here to end this once and for all."

Theresa sized up the situation and leaned into Camilla, whispering as softly as she could. "He's here for you, I'm sure of it. Be prepared to kill him."

Camilla listened but didn't respond. She kept her eyes on the witch dangling in the air and the flame pointed at her throat.

"No need to come in here flames ablazing," Theresa stated, back to her controlling voice, which was in stark contrast to her appearance. She spoke like someone in control, years of practice at the art of deception serving her in this moment. But it was a thin façade. She looked like an escapee from the mental ward. "Collette isn't exactly in my good graces, but she needn't be a pawn when this is just between us."

Shane slowly let Collette down to the ground, gently resting her upon her feet without touching her at all. The flame he sucked back to his hands, but he kept a fireball at the ready. "I agree that this is just between us, and I have no issue with any witch that doesn't have an issue with me."

Theresa gestured at the black hooded figures following closely behind Shane. "And you turn down my offer to work together but side with these witches?"

Kara stepped forward and pulled her hood down to reveal herself, but a ray of sunlight caught her and her cheek scorched. She kept her hood down but walked over to Collette to remain in the shadows of the cardboard boxes. Collette was still hurt from her just-healed broken leg but was otherwise unharmed. She stood near Kara with no trace of fear, curious about what would happen next.

Theresa sucked in a gasp of air. "Vampires. In witches' robes? And you brought my own beautiful daughter here to use against me again?"

"Stepdaughter," Kara corrected, standing defiantly. "And I came on my own."

Theresa let out a shrill laugh, still trying to

sound as if nothing was bothering her, but she was doing a poor job of it. "So you bring a handful of monsters into a witch's coven and expect what? For us to be scared?"

"If you and Camilla come quietly with us, no one else needs to get hurt," Shane announced, bouncing the fireball from palm to palm. Isabelle hissed behind him. She didn't want to leave without a fight, but Shane really didn't want to hurt anyone but Theresa. There had been too much retaliation on both sides already.

Theresa lifted her chin. She wasn't going down without a fight either. "We're not going anywhere with you. Now be gone. We are in mourning."

"Theresa, at every turn you have proven that you can't be trusted." Shane stepped forward. Theresa and Camilla both stood their ground. Luke, Isabelle and Julianna also stepped forward.

Kara remained in the shadows only so she wouldn't have to put her hood up just yet. But if it came to it, she would gladly cover her face and fight. Right now she wanted to look on Theresa, the woman who had murdered her mother and forced her and her sister into a dark world, and to have Theresa look back and see her face.

"If you take one more step, we will be forced to hurt you. Again," Theresa announced. Some witches took fighting stances just in case.

Camilla stared on, still impassive.

Shane boldly took another step forward. There wasn't much he was afraid of in this room. He stared at Theresa, fireball still in hand, as he approached her.

"Witches!" she yelled. "Attack!"

But no one moved.

"Looks like everybody is through taking orders from you," Emily stepped out of the shadows at the other end of the salon near the red door. Henna was right behind her and Elias only a few steps behind.

"Oh, Emily, thank goodness. I was worried about you," Theresa declared.

"Only because you want me as your pawn. We are all your pawns." Emily gestured at the coven. "But it's over, Theresa. We don't want to be minions in your political games anymore."

Theresa waved her hand in Emily's direction. "You've been a witch for all of a week. You don't know what you want."

"We want you to leave and never come back to Ventura," Emily stated flatly. Kara watched on with pride. Her sister had always been vapid, more into fashion than fighting. This was a new side to her and it made Kara beam. It looked like her sister had more to offer this world than make-up and fashion, after all. Once Theresa was taken care of, they would be quite the duo—witch and vampire.

"This is ridiculous," Theresa announced. "Go join your sister with the vampires then. But don't pretend to speak for the whole coven."

"I think you should step down too," Henna announced. If she was still nervous and afraid, she didn't let it show. She was a trained witch of the Harbor Coven, after all. Hide your emotions. That's the ace in your sleeve.

"You'll get no argument from me," Collette

announced, standing near Kara and the pile of warehouse boxes.

Kara smiled at her, brandishing her fangs.

"Well." Theresa put her hands on her hips. She had expected something from Shane, maybe even Kara and Emily, but betrayal from some of her well-trained witches was new for her. "If that's how you three feel, then allow me to retort." To Camilla she whispered, "Get ready." To the room, she announced again, "This is *my* coven. I'm not stepping down from what I built. If you don't want to be a part of it anymore, then leave."

And then to punctuate her words, she swept her arms toward the back of the room, where Collette stood with Kara, all the way to where Emily, Henna and Elias stood near the front. As she did, she sent an unseen force to knock them all back. Some fell, some just slid, witches and vampires alike. Only Shane remained standing and unmoved by her actions.

And he threw his fireball at the ground, watching as it blazed a trail from where he stood straight to Theresa and Camilla.

Deep down he'd always known Theresa wouldn't make this easy. Shane knew what had to be done. And it was time to do it.

14

The trail of fire shot across the floor, emanating light and heat as it went. Suddenly this huge warehouse with tall ceilings felt very small. The fire was in the middle of the building in seconds, like someone had taken a match to a line of gun powder.

The witches standing behind Theresa near the workbench where all the potions were concocted watched aghast. They made no move to protect their unkempt leader or to stop the fire from burning down the warehouse. They simply watched on in amazement, as if this were a great show.

And Kara, Isabelle, Collette, and Luke in the back of the warehouse, and Emily, Henna and Elias from the front of the warehouse, were recovering from the power blast Theresa had hit them with. They had barely regained their footing when the blaze shot forth from Shane's hands.

The fighting had begun.

Very aware of the morning sunlight coming through the windows that lined the ceiling, the vampires kept their hoods up. Kara lifted her hood in preparation for having to enter the fray. Nothing was going to stop her from avenging her mother, even if Shane got soft. Isabelle smiled a deliciously wicked smile, fangs extended, under her black witch's hood. This is what she lived for and she was more than ready to end witches—or, at the very least, Theresa.

Collette, suddenly very aware that she was closer to adversaries than her sorority of witches, stepped a few feet away from Kara—not far enough to be back with the witches, but enough room to allow her to react if Kara turned on her. But Kara's eyes were on her stepmother. She would fight other witches if she needed to, but she wasn't here for anyone but Theresa. This was personal.

The flame that shot across the room was halted inches from Theresa by her counterspell. She blocked the advance of the flames, dousing it with a wave of her hand, and tried to send an offensive spell toward Shane. Her arms swung toward him and a force of air flew in his direction. He waved it away easily.

He took a step forward, sunlight from the windows above highlighting his skin and bouncing off him with no reaction. The less sun-resistant vampires in hooded robes behind him followed his lead and stepped forward.

Theresa sent another spell, fighting fire with fire by creating her own fireball and sending it to Shane. His pants lit up with the flame from Theresa's spell. But it was short-lived. With a flick of his wrist, water fell from his hand and put the fire out. His pants were singed a bit, but otherwise no harm was done.

He took another step forward, and so did Isabelle, Luke and Kara.

Again Theresa went on the offensive. This time she aimed for Isabelle—not wanting to hurt Kara. She still harbored the desire to kill Kara and resurrect her as a human just as she had done to Julianna. She would need to be in Kara's good graces. She sent a blast of energy toward Isabelle that would have blown her out the back door. Except Shane saw it coming, so he used his power to lift Isabelle out of the way, and the spell went barreling past her and knocked out the door in the back of the warehouse.

"Damn," Isabelle said, realizing how close she'd come to also being blown out the back door. "I'm going to enjoy ripping your throat out, you bitch."

And Shane again stepped forward, slowly closing in on Theresa. He didn't need to rush. He didn't believe without her witches fighting back that she was any match for his power. He reached forward and used his energy to lift Theresa into the air. She countered with energy of her own and was able to escape his unseen grasp. She fell to the ground and watched Shane take another step forward.

"Witches!" she instructed the Harbor Coven. "Take out the others. Leave Shane for me."

One or two witches got into fighting stances, but most didn't move at all. Camilla watched on like a spectator. Shane just shook his head.

"Did you not hear me?" Theresa screamed. "They are here to kill all of us. Our only hope is to fight."

Collette crossed her arms and shouted back. "They seem to be only interested in you. And this is your fight. Stop bringing us into wars you create for yourself."

No other witches said anything, but they seemed to agree with the general sentiment. Whether they were simply through following Theresa's leadership or they were afraid of dying like Elyse, they didn't feel the need to enter the battle unless they themselves were attacked.

And the vampires, and even the two witches who told them where to find her, were here only for Theresa.

Shane took another step forward. Theresa instinctively took a step back. She had never not had the support of the coven—*her* coven—before.

"Looks like it's down to you and me, Theresa," Shane smirked.

"I've killed worthier men than you, you little shit," Theresa spat back.

Kara stepped forward, her hood still up to protect her from the streaming sunlight. "You also killed my mother, so it's not just you and Shane."

Theresa looked at her stepdaughter and sensed easy prey—or at least easier than Shane was. She also felt the tiniest spark of hope that Kara would ever return to her fizzle out. The vampire before her hated her. She sent a spell hurling in Kara's direction. Again, Shane reacted quickly and moved Kara out of the way. The spell collided with the boxes behind Kara, and they shriveled quickly into piles of dust. Kara looked at the pile, the remnants of the spell that was meant for her, and then back to Theresa. "You bitch!"

"We're all sick of your games and the vampires you keep harming," Luke shouted to Theresa.

"And I'm here hoping it all goes south so I get to kill something," Isabelle sneered from underneath her robe.

"Last chance, Theresa," Shane shouted. "Leave quietly with us."

Theresa snarled and sent another fireball at him. He doused it with water midair. She tried to lift him with her energy. He shoved it away with his own. She tried an immobilization spell. He blocked it.

Theresa was getting frustrated. Without her coven, she wasn't able to do much against Shane. But next to her stood his weakness. Quietly, calmly, watching everything without saying a word.

Camilla.

Her hands were still folded in front of her. What a pretty little flower. She didn't seem worried or afraid with spells and powers being used all around her.

Theresa realized in her emotional state that she was fighting with the wrong weapons. Shane couldn't be harmed easily. He was a vampire who could walk in sunlight, control the elements, block spells with his hands, know your movements before you did them.

But his heart was another thing entirely.

And how well she knew that love was always a weakness. His heart was fragile, sitting in a glass box and Theresa knew she could easily smash it. He'd do anything to protect the young witch he thought was his girlfriend. Men! So easily undone by pretty faces.

Theresa grabbed Camilla by her throat and pulled her in front of herself to block her body from Shane's advances. Sure enough, he froze instantly, just as she'd expected him to.

"Let me go or Camilla dies," Theresa shouted to Shane over Camilla's head. It didn't go unnoticed that Camilla looked frightened for the first time that morning. She still made no sound, but her eyes were brimming with fear.

"I know she can't be killed because of the spell you all took," Shane tried to sound confident, but the slightest bit of doubt was lacing his words. He needed to call Theresa's bluff, but he wouldn't let Camilla be another tragedy to Theresa's mind games.

"You fool! I made that spell. You think I can't undo it?" Theresa shouted. Then to Camilla she said,

"Use it now, Camilla. The gift you gave him. End this."
And to show how serious she was that she wanted Camilla to kill Shane, she squeezed harder on Camilla's throat. True, she might not die from it, but she still felt the pain and she still struggled to get oxygen.

Camilla looked at Shane and saw the handsome man with blonde curls who had taken her in and invited her trust. He was worried now, but not about himself. He worried for Camilla. She knew that. She also felt Theresa's fingers and knew that she meant what she said. This was Camilla's moment to prove her loyalty and show her worth. She *had* masterminded the whole plan that led to this moment—Theresa had been completely right about that.

Camilla was a good little witch. And Theresa had taught her well.

"Let me go so I can," Camilla croaked to Theresa.

"Let Camilla go and no one else gets hurt," Shane shouted. "We'll leave quietly."

"Bullshit!" Isabelle shouted, but Theresa just smiled and eased up on Camilla's throat.

"Shane, I have to do this," Camilla said, looking straight at him.

"We'll leave, you can come with us. You don't have to do what she says," Shane answered, eyes locked with Camilla's. They both barely registered that there were others in the room, some wanting to fight, some wanting to flee, but watching the events unfold, unable to tear away from watching Camilla's treachery.

Luke looked between the two and a complete foreboding filled him. "You hurt him, Camilla, and I will spend the rest of my days making sure you pay."

Camilla ignored him. She kept staring at Shane.

"Do it, Camilla. Now," Theresa instructed again. This was her ace in the hole. What would the vampires be without Shane? Without him, their annihilation would be effortless.

"Do you still have the hex bag I gave you?" Camilla called to Shane.

He nodded, slowly pulling the bag out from a pocket. He held it in front of himself in the middle of his palm.

"And do you trust me?" Camilla asked, her eyes locked on Shane's.

Theresa giggled behind Camilla.

"No!" Isabelle shouted, sensing this was all going badly and not in the way she'd hoped. "Don't do it, Shane."

"You know I do," Shane answered.

"Then burn it."

Without the slightest hesitation, he did as she instructed. The fire started in the center of his palm just below the hex bag, sending it up in flames quickly, black smoke swirling from his palm to the high warehouse ceiling.

And the scream was piercing. The pain immense, not just from the physical pain but also the emotional pain of betrayal.

The minute the pain began, Theresa knew. Her poisonous flower and good little witch had done as she'd been taught. She'd held her emotions close to her vest and tricked her adversary. Only Theresa had been wrong about who the adversary was.

Theresa began to transmogrify before their very eyes.

Witches and vampires alike watched in horror as Theresa went from a beautiful young woman, to a middle-aged woman, and then to an old woman. Her skin began to sallow and wrinkle, her hair to turn gray and scraggly. She physically shriveled, from someone standing tall to a hunched-back elderly woman. She looked every bit the part of an old witch from a scary movie.

But it didn't stop there.

She continued to transform. Her eyes and cheeks got more sunken, her body became more bony, and her hair continued to grow, gray and scraggly. Theresa continued to scream as she went from old woman to walking corpse. Her skin slowly eroded and peeled away from her bones. And it kept going. She pulled at her face and hair as if she could stop the spell with her hands, but it was no use.

Starting at her head, her bones began to turn to powder, crumbling before them in a pile of ashes to ashes, dust to dust. The screaming stopped and the room fell eerily silent.

Theresa was gone and left only a pile of dust on the floor to remind them that she'd ever existed.

Camilla ran to Shane and threw her arms around his neck. He scooped her up in his arms and returned the embrace warmly.

Finally, it was Isabelle who broke the silence. "What the hell just happened?"

Camilla broke from her embrace with Shane to explain. She raised her voice so everyone could know. "The ultimate undo spell. I've been working on it for years. It completely erases all magic its victim has done to themselves. In this case, it returned Theresa to her rightful age of four-hundred years old."

"Holy shit," Luke said.

Shane sent a fireball to the dusty remains of Theresa. He couldn't take the chance that anyone would keep the ashes and try to resurrect her or something. Who knew what these witches could or would do?

"So, what happens now?" Emily asked. She,

Henna and Elias walked over to join the vampires, Elias being very careful to walk the long way to avoid the sunlight.

"I can't believe she's gone," Emily said. She was shocked and relieved at the same time. So much had changed in Emily over the course of the past few weeks when her world had gone from football games and homecoming dances to the underworld and dark magic. And now, indirectly, she had blood on her hands. Her own stepmother. But she couldn't bring herself to feel guilty. There was too much freedom for her family in Theresa's undoing.

"So, you were on the vampire's side all the time?" Collette asked Camilla.

"I only wanted to be free of Theresa's reign. I never chose vampires over witches or vice versa." Shane slipped his hand into Camilla's as she spoke to her coven. "I hope that you'll all forgive me for the role I played."

"Forgive you?" Henna asked. "We thank you. We disagreed with everything she was putting us through, and Elyse's death was the final straw." Henna quickly turned to Shane to explain. "We don't blame you for her death. We blame Theresa. She was obsessed with killing Kara so we could resurrect her as human. The rest of us just wanted things to be as they were."

"No way," Kara said, shaking her head under her robe. "I'm never going back."

"And you don't have to." Emily walked over to her sister and hugged her. Kara hesitantly hugged her sister back. She was still a newborn, after all, and her sister smelled delicious. "We all are what we are. Why should that keep us fighting?"

"As far as I'm concerned, it's all over," Shane explained. He almost glowed standing there in the sunlight. No one could ever mistake him for 'just another guy.' He was majestic. "And Emily, our home is your home. You're welcome to come live with us in the compound." He turned to the coven, still in awe of the morning's events. "That goes for all of you. Anyone who wants to live with us is welcome, and we offer you our protection to practice your craft however you choose."

There was another murmur, mostly a hum of excitement amongst the Harbor Coven. Camilla threw her arms around Shane's neck again. And into his ear, she whispered, "Let's go home."

Nuzzled into her neck and under her hair, Shane whispered back, "I like hearing you say that." He pulled away from Camilla and spoke to the gathering once more. "All who are coming, let's go."

He started to pull away from Camilla and head to the back door, but she pulled his hand back with a smirk. "You know, you are in a coven? You don't need to go on foot."

Shane smiled back and gestured to the beautiful brunette before him. "By all means, transport us home, little witch."

15

"So we've ended the Dark Prophecy then." Shane spoke aloud to his council. "Theresa is dead and she's the one who planned to annihilate vampires."

It had been a few days since the deaths of their two main foes, Dimas and Theresa. It felt as if a huge weight had been lifted off their shoulders, and yet no one much felt like celebrating. The prophecy always remained looming over them, dark and daunting.

"Maybe the prophecy was never even real." Luke shrugged. "I know I started to believe when you showed your powers, Shane, but maybe it was more coincidence than prediction. Maybe we took events and made them fit the prophecy instead of the other way around? The whole crap prophecy does sound like hogwash."

Johann rested his hand under his chin, a sort of thinking pose. "That's possible, I suppose. But it's likely foolish to dismiss it so easily. We are most easily preyed upon by that which we do not see coming."

They were back in the basement of the former Strashni compound. Camilla had begun making some design changes and making the room feel less like a prison. Dimas had always wanted people to not feel welcome, to limit their stay. Camilla, however, wanted this room to feel more like a Presidential cabinet, with Shane as leader and his vampire advisors as the cabinet members. The walls were painted a cream color so it wouldn't feel so "heavy," and large leather sectionals had been added so there was plenty of seating for all. She'd also added a large, regal desk and coffee tables so they could take notes if needed.

"I think"—Regina sat on Alexi's lap and toyed with his hair—"that something is coming. We don't know when and we may not know how, but it will. If the first half of the prophecy came true, why on earth would we dismiss the second half so readily?"

"Then we fight," Isabelle stood with the energy she couldn't keep contained. "If we're going down, we go down swinging."

Shane nodded. "If it comes to that, we will Isabelle. And you can lead the troops to battle. But I think we're going to need more details about what the supposed threat is." He turned to the oldest vampire on the council. "Johann, how much do you know about the Dark Prophecy?"

Johann shook his head. "Not much more than what I told you before. Slowly, but surely vampires begin to disappear. I'm not convinced it's anything you *can* fight."

"But there must be a way to stop it." Elias leaned back on the couch, his long black hair uncharacteristically let loose.

Johann smirked and gestured to Shane. "There was no way to stop *him*."

"But Shane is the most powerful vampire,

maybe even being, on the planet."   Isabelle was practically shouting. "Whatever it is, he can stop it."

"Not if the prophecy is to be believed," Luke interjected. He was leaning forward on his knees and looked over at Shane. They rarely needed to say anything to one another, they were so on the same wavelength. Luke believed in Shane and he was only half-convinced the prophecy was real, but doubts plagued his mind. Shane understood. He had doubts too.

"What about the witches?" Camilla spoke softly and all eyes turned toward her. She sat toward the front near Shane, her legs folded underneath her. Up until now she hadn't spoken.

"I think you know that we all don't share Shane's kindness toward your nasty kind," Regina sneered. Her face was full of disgust. "I've always said I think the witches are behind the plague that eradicates our kind."

No one said anything for fear of offending Shane, but you could tell from the expressions on many vampire faces that Regina was not alone in her sentiments.

Luke felt the need to defend Shane's position. "Shane made sure the witches are our allies now. They wouldn't kill us."

Shane put a calming hand on Luke's arm. He appreciated the support, but he knew better than to write off a potential threat. Theresa had been a witch, after all. "We know witches can be very powerful, and while we have allies, I am sure we still have enemies. I don't think *all* witches are the enemy, but I will proceed cautiously."

"No," Camilla spoke up, looking only at Shane. "I meant what if witches could stop the second part of the prophecy from coming true?"

Regina snorted haughtily, but no one else made a sound.

"I'm listening," Shane urged her to explain.

"Well." Camilla took his hand in hers, still avoiding contact with any other vampire in the dimly lit room. "We know our spells work against your kind, and we have protection spells that allow our mortal bodies to become immortal. It might take some trial and error, but I think we can make a spell to protect you." She swallowed and looked at the floor. "I think I can make that spell."

"I trust you." Shane kissed her forehead and saw that her eyes were brimming with held-back tears.

"I don't want to lose you." Her voice was barely above a whisper.

Regina groaned loudly. "This is ridiculous. I can't even take her seriously. Please just turn her so I don't have to sit here fighting the urge to rip her throat out anymore."

Luke laughed and Shane shot him down with a glare. Luke sat back and put his arms up. "What? She *does* smell delicious."

"Okay, the topic of Camilla's non-vampire state is not the business of this council." Shane shut down the group with a stern voice and a powerful glower. "How do we learn more about this plague? We have to know what it is before we can stop it."

Johann sat forward, as serious as ever. "I know

who we can talk to. She's a very old vampire living up north."

Damian, who up until now had been watching the conversation but not actively participating, sat straight up and turned to Johann. "Are you talking about Bianca?"

"This conversation just keeps going from bad to worse," Regina groaned again.

Luke looked at Shane, his mouth agape, and then back to Johann. "*Bianca* Bianca?"

Johann nodded. "If anyone has the answers you seek, it will be her."

Damian shook his head. "Good luck to that traveling party."

Shane looked around. "What am I missing?"

No one spoke for a minute, so Luke felt the need to clue Shane in. "Bianca is so evil, she even feeds on other vampires. Trust me when I say *she's* the mold for every Hollywood movie about creatures of the night. If there's a vampire on this planet that has a direct connection to hell, it's Bianca."

"I spoke to her many years ago, and she was ancient in those days. And, no, her bedside manner is not...pleasant, but I believe she will have the information we need to stop the rest of the Dark Prophecy from coming true." Johann looked around the room at the concerned faces looking back at him.

Shane nodded. He'd faced evil in his short second life. If he had to do it again, so be it. "Very well. I'll put a team together to go talk to Bianca."

Isabelle put a hand on Shane's shoulder. "Finally, something exciting happens around here. When do we leave?"

"Isabelle." Damian spoke like a punishing father. "Bianca eats hotheads like you for breakfast. And I mean that quite literally."

"I understand where Isabelle is coming from." Elias stood up next to the feisty vampire. "Some of us are soldiers. We just need a mission. A purpose. Something to fight for. Shane, I'd be honored to face Bianca with you."

"And I'd feel better if you were by my side."

Shane nodded up to Elias. Then he turned back to Johann. "How many should I take with me?"

"You could take twenty of your finest warriors and I'd still worry about your safety." Johann spoke with an air of caution. "She likely won't be expecting your powers, though, so you can use the element of surprise to catch her off guard."

"Then I'll gather all who want to join me, and we'll leave one week from today. In the meantime, we'll rest up, feed and prepare."

"Well, I'll give you one thing, Shaney." Regina leaned forward, allowing her ample bosom to be on full display. "From nasty witches to cantankerous old vampires, you sure are adventurous with the women in your life."

Luke leaned back and laughed heartily, but Camilla just pursed her lips and glared.

Shane ignored Regina. In his short life as ruler of these creatures, he had only wanted to be fair and keep everyone safe. It simply couldn't be done without facing certain darknesses. No one had the powers he had. And it was up to him alone to get the answers needed to save them all.

Sometimes the crown was heavy on the head. He knew that. But this was what he was born to do. And, whether or not he liked it, no one could do it for him.

16

"So, what do you want to do? Go home?" Shane sat on the patio with Julianna, his feet up on the chair before him. The bright midday sun overpowered their senses and they both squinted to be able to see each other. Julianna's blonde curls reflected the light with a golden sheen. It had been so long since they'd sat in the sun together, Shane instantly felt like a ten-year-old boy again.

"Nah, I can't go back. That life has ended." Julianna squinted in response to her brother.

"I found your journal. Sorry to say, I've read it many times."

"My journal?" If Julianna was offended, she hid it well. Her face reflected surprise that something so trivial still existed. "What are you doing with that?"

"I used to read it when you died from your first human life. When you'd become a vampire. And then I went back home and got it again when I lost you again. I practically have it memorized." Shane stared at the ground. It felt good to be honest, but he did feel slightly guilty for the invasion of privacy.

Julianna laughed at the thought of what frivolities must exist in her old journal from two lifetimes ago. "That must be an entertaining read."

"That's why I wondered where you might want to go with your new lease on life. You spoke of travel in your journal."

Julianna looked off into the distance as she answered. "Luke wants me to stay here."

Shane laughed. "In a house full of vampires? I don't think so."

Julianna fought back the urge to laugh along with him. "Don't you think I'll blend in? With all the witches that live here now? Mine surely can't be the tastiest blood."

"Jules, I don't know if it's safe for you to be with Luke. You're so vulnerable now," Shane pleaded with his sister.

"I might be human, but I know more about being a vampire than you do." Julianna rolled her eyes at her brother. "Give me some credit."

Shane sighed. "It would be nice to have you around. It really broke my heart to lose you twice."

"And I've been meaning to say I'm sorry." Julianna lowered her voice and her eyes fell to the stone patio beneath them. It was a warm day, but a cool breeze kept the temperature nice and comfortable.

"Sorry? For what?

"For trusting Dimas. I should have protected you from him and instead I took you straight to him." Julianna shook her head, trying to erase the memory and the guilt.

"There's nothing to be sorry for. You had no way of knowing he was the betrayer of the vampires." Shane squeezed his sister's hand.

"He wanted me to be his mistress, did you know

that?"

"Gross." Shane couldn't hide the repulsion on his face. The thought of the smarmy albino vampire lusting after his sister was enough to make him nauseous, and vampires don't get nauseous easily. "Better not let Luke hear that."

"Or what? He'll kill him again?" Julianna smirked at her brother.

The sound of laughter from the sliding glass door alerted them and they both turned to see Emily with her arm around her vampire sister. Happiness and love filled their faces as they walked past.

"I don't think the prophecy completely got it right," Julianna announced.

Shane looked quizzically at his sister. "How so?"

"The most powerful vampire to ever roam the earth didn't just unite vampires. You united witches and vampires. No one could see that coming." Julianna shook her head.

"I think we're natural allies." Shane sat back on the patio chair and let the sun warm his cheeks. Being able to withstand sunlight was one power he hoped he never took for granted.

"So did Dimas."

Shane shot Julianna a look. He didn't like to be compared to Dimas. So Julianna added an explanation. "My point is others may have tried. You succeeded. The prophecy missed that. That's a power no one saw coming."

"Speaking of prophecy, I'm going to visit a vampire called Bianca next week." Shane looked over at Julianna. "Ever heard of her?"

"Yeah." Julianna's eyes widened at the mention of the name. "I heard never to go anywhere near her. Why would you need to go see her?"

"Johann thinks she might have the answers we need to stop the annihilation of vampires. Apparently, there's a second part to the prophecy and it doesn't end well for us."

Julianna crossed her legs, staring at the greenery all around them in the backyard. She smoothed her long, black skirt and then folded her hands on her lap. "What if you just walked away?"

"Walked away? What are you talking about?" Shane sat forward. He cleared his mind to sense Julianna's thoughts. She stared back as he saw a vision of the two of them, just as they looked today except both were human.

"If it worked for me, it could work for you," Julianna replied. "You have yourself a little witch who can resurrect you. And you won't have to worry about the annihilation of vampires as you and Camilla go live a long and happy human life."

Shane thought about her words.

Could it be that simple? Could he just walk away? But then what about Luke, Isabelle and Kara? They were counting on him. A sense of honor wouldn't allow him to abandon the ones he loved.

"I can't. At least not until I stop the Prophecy and know that everyone is safe."

"Then I'm in." Julianna stood and reached for her brother to stand with her. She shook her head and let her long hair bounce along her back. "Let's stop the

Prophecy and then go live as humans on a little farm somewhere."

"A farm?" Shane had to laugh at the vision of himself, Julianna, Camilla and Luke in a post-vampire existence tending to something as mundane as a farm.

Julianna laughed with him. "It just sounded peaceful. What about a private island?"

"Ooooh, or a remote cabin in Alaska."

They walked back toward the sliding glass door that led to the compound. It was late morning, so many vampires had already gone to their death sleep. The home was still and quiet.

Smiling up at her brother, Julianna suggested, "Or sail from port to port on a yacht?"

"I like it," Shane nodded. "What about a beach in Mexico? Something tells me ex-vampires would be accepted in that community."

Shane slid the door open. Sunlight was shining into the hallway, but just next to the hallway, hiding in the shadows, stood an imposing figure. Shane froze in the doorway, Julianna at his side. It was Luke, tall and muscular, arms crossed in front of his chest. It was the expression on his face that gave Shane pause. He didn't have to use any psychic powers to know something was horribly wrong. Luke was normally jovial and sarcastic. His eyes had worry in them.

"Isabelle?" Shane asked, immediately sensing she was at the heart of Luke's update.

"There's no easy way to say this, Shane." Luke frowned as he spoke. "She's gone. She left at daybreak to go find Bianca."

"What? How is she traveling in the day?" Shane asked, but the second the words left his mouth, he knew the answer and it hit him in his gut like a sucker punch. He leaned against the wall for support.

Julianna ran to her brother but looked up at Luke. "What's going on, Luke?"

"She took Camilla with her. The two of them went off together, by themselves, to face the most evil vampire in recorded history." Luke's handsome face was creased with worry. It was clear he didn't have high hopes for a successful mission.

"Why?" Julianna asked, still trying to fit all the pieces together.

She was still looking at Luke, but it was Shane who answered. "Isabelle didn't want to wait. And Camilla was trying to protect me by facing her without me." He put his hand on his forehead. "Shit!"

"I'd ask what you want to do, but I already know the answer. I packed a backpack for us," Luke replied, still avoiding the sunlight.

"Wake Elias. We're leaving now," Shane ordered. He turned to Julianna, but she responded before he could instruct her.

"I know, I know. I'm human so I need to stay behind." Julianna held her hands up innocently. "You two come back safely, okay?"

Her brother kissed her forehead and then he picked up the backpack on the floor next to Luke. Julianna walked over to Luke and slipped her arms around his waist, resting her head on his chest. He squeezed her back and then kissed her softly on the lips before running upstairs to get Elias.

It wasn't quite the original plan, but like it or not, it was now in motion. It was time to face Bianca. Step one in ending the Dark Prophecy.

To Be Concluded in Episode 3: *Deliverance from the Prophecy*

No one expected there was more to the Prophecy, and now a witch and a vampire have gone rogue to stop it on their own by facing one of the oldest - and known to be the most evil - vampire of recent memory. But Shane knows that only he has the powers needed to face such a powerful adversary and live. First he'll have to save his friends - and then he'll have to save them all by stopping the very Prophecy that made him who he is.